POWER

— TO THE —

Princess

Lincoln
Children's Books

Dear Reader,

A few months ago, I had the pleasure of attending the Noble Monarch Jubilee, a special conference for leaders from Fairyland to meet, share successes and swap ideas. It was there that I met some of the princesses featured in this book.

Belle, undercover agent of the Fairyland police, spoke on a panel with Cinderella about income equality and crime prevention. Aurora (otherwise known as Sleeping Beauty) and Snow White gave a talk about body image and the science of sleep. Rapunzel gave a sneak peek of her cutting edge inclusive design tools. The programming was top-notch and highlighted the hard work of these royal leaders, their fun personalities and their amazing potential. However, it was the conversation away from the spotlight that captured my attention. After the book signing session I overheard the princesses talking amongst themselves.

"I wish our fans knew the truth about us," said Sleeping Beauty.

"I know, it's so annoying," Belle the Brave complained. "Everyone thinks we just marry princes and live happily ever after."

"You're telling me. I'm tired of autographing glass shoes. That's not what being a princess is about," agreed Cinderella.

"But how can we show people more of who we really are?" asked the Little Mermaid.

As the princesses talked, I could tell there was something missing from their stories. "I think I might be able to help you," I interrupted. "I'm an author, and if you're interested, I could write a book about you."

Luckily for me, the princesses were into the idea. That day, we talked a lot about their stories, and what it means to be a princess. They taught me that a princess is a person who seeks to help others, is open to learning new things, and who looks for ways to add purpose to their own lives and to the lives of those around them.

Over the following months, I interviewed the princesses to discover their unique stories. Each one told me about where they were from, and of a time when they or a family member or friend faced a big challenge. Often there was magic or mystery. Sometimes a daring adventure or a quest. And always funny moments and surprises too.

What struck me the most was that every princess I met reminded me of someone I knew. My friends, my family, people I've worked with: athletes and artists, teachers and scientists, parents and kids. I believe the characters in the princesses' stories will remind you of people you know too. Maybe the princesses make the same mistakes or have the same triumphs, take the same risks or face similar challenges.

Now that their stories have been retold, turn the pages and get reacquainted with these powerful princesses. Maybe like I did, you'll recognise some of your own story too!

Vita Murrow

Noble Monarch Jubilee

LIST OF ATTENDEES AND THEIR STORIES

Belle the Brave

Once upon a time, in a sunny French province, there lived a girl called Belle. Belle the Brave to be precise, because Belle was fearless.

What is fearless? Fearless is breathing deeply when you must get a vaccination at the doctor's. Fearless is walking proudly through a tangle of spider webs. Fearless is jumping from high rocks into cold water. And in Belle's case, fearless meant venturing into a scary forest, when no one else would even consider it. (The place was called the Forbidden Forest, after all.)

It all started one bright and cheery day, when Belle's father had to go on a trip. Each of his daughters had a special request.

"Can you bring me back a set of paper and paints?" asked one.

"Winter is coming. I'll have a warm hat if you spot one," asked the other.

"Belle, what can I bring you?" her father asked. But Belle was busy, studying her map of the Forbidden Forest.

"Oh, you know me, nothing special. Maybe a flower?"

The sisters happily waved their father on his way. But after a few days passed, and their father hadn't returned, they began to worry. Days turned to a week, and finally Belle realised she alone would need to go in search of him, alone. For among her sisters, she was the best tree climber, cobweb walker and rocky-ledge jumper. Plus, she had been working on her Forbidden Forest map and this was just

the opportunity to try it out.

"Are you sure you should be doing this?" fretted Belle's sisters. "It's nearly dark and what about the. . . you know. . . monsters?"

"Monsters bonsters," said Belle. "I'll be perfectly fine." She gave her sisters a big kiss and squeeze and set off – just as brave as you please – into the night. Soon the call of owls welcomed her as she ventured into the Forbidden Forest.

The trail grew thick and brambly, and Belle drew out her trusty map for guidance. An expert tracker and navigator, Belle was quick to identify a route. But as luck would have it, a flash of lightning felled a tree right in her path!

"Ugh!" Belle moaned, because the tree was too big to climb over, even for her. However, the forest heard her sigh, and the next flash of lightning illuminated another path, leading away from the main one. "Alright!" thought Belle. She'd always suspected the Forbidden Forest had some good hidden secrets.

Belle followed this new path and was soon brought to the foot of a great and mysterious castle. It was shrouded in fog, veiled by glistening snow, and circled by an immense rose garden. It nearly took Belle's breath away, but she did manage one word of marvel: "Wow."

Belle climbed nearly a hundred stairs to reach the door. As she leaned against it to catch her breath, the mighty latch gave way, and the door swung open to reveal

a great hall. It was dark and freezing cold, without a soul in sight. Belle stepped inside and was just about to call out when the door closed behind her with a great thud, and a large shadow took its place.

As Belle turned around she could see that the shadow belonged to an enormous creature. Overgrown and clumsy, with terrible posture and likely terrible breath, too. A beast, really. Belle could also make out someone's feet behind the Beast, so she called out, "Papa, is that you?"

An exhausted heap of a man was collapsed at the Beast's feet. Belle could see that her father was weak and sick. Also, that he was clutching a once-lovely stem of roses.

"Gracious!" exclaimed Belle to the Beast. "Can't you see he's unwell? Don't just stand there, help me out."

Belle pulled her father up and found him a soft chair to sit in. She hurried to the hearth to set about making a fire. "What are you doing?" she said to the Beast, who was standing like a stunned statue. "Bring in some dry wood, would you?"

"I'd like you to leave!" the Beast bellowed. "Your father was sneaking around on my property, and I'm not one for guests. He is now my prisoner!"

The shouting stirred Belle's father. "Belle, what on earth are you doing here?" he gasped. "Get out while you still can. This is no place for you!"

"I'll be the judge of th—"

"I caught this man stealing from my rose garden," the Beast roared as he pulled Belle's father to his feet, "so one of you is going to pay for it with your freedom!"

"Oh, don't you threaten me!" Belle shot back. "Put my father down right now!" The astonished Beast let Belle's father fall back into the chair. Belle got right in the Beast's face. "Now here's my counter-offer," she said. "You let my father go, and I'll stay here to repay his debt."

And so, it was agreed. Belle would stay on as a guest of the Beast. As days turned into weeks, and weeks turned into months, it wasn't all cupcakes and sprinkles, but it also wasn't all thorns and nettles, either. It was true: the Beast was a real grouch and terrible host, and kept himself to himself. Yet Belle knew things weren't always as scary as they might first appear.

One day, both the Beast and Belle arrived in the larder at the same time for a snack. They reached for the cookie spread at just the same moment, and the Beast – in a gentler mood than normal – quickly withdrew his hand and made to leave the room.

"Wait," Belle said. "Grab me a spoon – we'll split it." The Beast hesitated at the door and then, to Belle's surprise, turned around, spoon in hand. They sat together for tea, enjoying the cookie spread to the last dollop, and finding, surprisingly, that they had lots to talk about.

"Oh, don't you threaten me!"

"Maybe we should do this again sometime?" said the Beast, shyly.

Belle smiled. They kept the cookie-dough tradition week after week. In one of their sessions, it turned out that the Beast was a great swing dancer. He taught Belle and they had hours of fun in the ballroom.

One day, the Beast came to Belle with a most unusual request. "I think I need a haircut," he said. "Spending time with you has helped me feel so much better about myself, and I think I'd like to look better, too."

"Why, of course!" said Belle. When she finished with the Beast, he had a dashing coif complete with a bun, groomed beard and even trimmed eyebrows.

"I love it!" exclaimed the Beast. "And I love you!" he added.

Belle was pleasantly surprised, for she too loved the Beast. But not as surprised as she was by what followed. For after the Beast spoke, a great flash of light filled the room, as though a firework had been set off. Tiny dazzling baubles of light rained down around them, and as they fell upon the Beast, he was transformed into – *tada!* – just a regular guy.

"Whaaaaaaat. . .?" said Belle.

The Beast looked sheepish. "I guess I have some explaining to do," he said. "Some time ago I was a prince and the victim of a curse. But before you feel sorry for me, I deserved it. I didn't always think about other people. In fact, sometimes I didn't even see past my own nose. I guess you could have called me—"

"Selfish?" offered Belle.

"Oh, I was more than selfish, and it caught up with me. One day a fairy arrived at the palace and needed my help. I – of course – couldn't be bothered. When I turned her away she turned me into a beast."

"That sounds a bit harsh," said Belle. "Curses never helped anyone."

"She said I would return to my true self when I could see the good in others, and then find someone who could see the good in me,"

the Prince continued.

Belle nodded. "Well, now you've changed back. Are you going to miss being a beast? There were some pretty cool things you could do."

"I'm glad to be myself again. But I learned a lot being a beast, and those lessons will stay with me. I hope you'll stay with me, too?" the Prince said hopefully.

"I can't think of anywhere I'd rather be," said Belle. "But first, I'd like to confront this 'fairy' you speak of. Curses are a crime best left in the past, and she should be held accountable."

In the morning, the Prince helped Belle map out a journey to find the fairy. Once again, she set off into the Forbidden Forest, which now felt like home. Belle's sharp navigating instincts brought her quickly to the fairy, who reluctantly went with Belle to the Fairyland Police.

As Belle made to leave the law enforcement station, a high-ranking detective called out to her. "Hey there, was it you who solved the curse at the Beast's castle?"

"Why, yes," said Belle, reaching for the door.

"That cold case eluded us for years. I couldn't get a single detective to brave the grounds. May I ask, weren't you at all afraid?" she pressed.

"Afraid of what?" asked Belle.

The detective smiled. "Can you stay for a minute? I think we have a job you'd be perfect for."

From that day forward, armed with a badge, her bravery and generous spirit, Belle worked tirelessly at the Fairyland Protection Office of Restorative Justice to protect the community from curses. She reached out to misunderstood magical creatures and helped build bridges between all the corners of the kingdom.

Belle was given the undercover name of 'Beauty' because of her ability to see the beauty in everyone and everything. At home in the castle, she and the Prince continued to enjoy jars of cookie spread. As their affection grew, the castle and gardens flourished, too.

One day, when the roses were in peak form, Belle mused, "These gardens would be perfect for a wedding."

The Prince agreed. "I know just the two people to celebrate," he added with a wink.

So, Belle and the Prince were married right there in that lovely spot, shortly thereafter. And that is how Belle became a princess.

The Little Mermaid

This story takes place in the depths of the ocean, in the kingdom of the Sea King. The Sea King was a commanding mer-person (a creature that is part-person and part-fish). In addition to his small but powerful kingdom, he ruled his six daughters. Their mother had died in an accident with a ship, so the King's mother lived with them and helped to raise the princesses.

The accident that took the King's wife broke his heart, and sadly it was put back together with fear. He had no tolerance for land dwellers and cautioned his daughters against learning anything about their customs. He often said cruel things about their above-sea neighbours, calling them 'dangerous, destructive, greedy and foul'. "Humans aren't worthy of your attention!" he'd bluster anytime the princesses showed interest in the human world.

From time to time, refuse, flotsam and relics of the world above drifted down to the sea kingdom. The King would make a big show of destroying these pollutants and invite an audience to watch as he bashed shipwrecks, buried treasures and ranted about the risks, dangers and ills that lay above. Because it distressed their father so, the princesses made it their business to keep the sea vegetation and plants healthy and free from the litter that crept down from the human world above them.

The youngest of the Sea King's daughters was called Marisha. Though she was the youngest, she was a natural leader. No pearls for this princess – she wore a fancy coat with tails (a tuxedo) that she salvaged during reef clean-up. In fact, Marisha had a solid collection of stuff from the world above, squirrelling away her discoveries and souvenirs before her father took note.

Sometimes Marisha's grandmother would tell her about the past, when the world of the mer-people and the world above were connected. But they had to keep their secret talks to themselves, because there was no telling how the Sea King would react if he knew.

Over the years, more and more litter from the world above plagued the sea kingdom. Machines and oddities sank into schools and other buildings. Ooze and slime clouded the waters. Many plants withered, the marine life struggled and some mer-people even resorted to wearing special masks. Marisha and her sisters found it hard to keep up with their clean-up projects.

The princesses urged their father the Sea King to venture above and learn more about the problem. If the land-dwellers knew what problems they were causing, maybe they would find a way to make the litter stop. But his heart was closed and his mind was shut tight as well.

*The youngest of the Sea King's daughters
was called Marisha.*

"Why would those creatures ever want to help?" he bellowed. "They care not a drop for us!" The King's anger sent great storms from the sea up to the surface of swirling sand, with raging currents and algae blooms.

When Marisha was nearly a grown-up, her grandmother told her of how, long ago, every mer-person before their sixteenth birthday was permitted to visit the land above. There they could share ideas, trade goods and learn about the human world. Marisha knew at once that this was what she wanted for her birthday. A reinstatement of the old ways! She was confident that if she knew what the world up there looked like, and how it worked, she could come up with a clean ocean plan.

On the morning of her birthday she tidied her cropped do, smoothed her jacket, and went to her father to appeal to him to visit the land above. She laid out her reasons calmly and clearly, but her father was not having it. Marisha could neither soften his heart nor open his mind and he forbade her from going to the surface.

But Marisha was defiant. The sea meant the world to her, and she would do whatever it took to restore the balance between the worlds joined at the horizon. So that night, Marisha snuck away and made her way to the surface.

As Marisha popped her head out of the water she spied an incredible sight. A three-masted ship sailed just a short distance away, and a great party was under way. It was a birthday party, for a princess just like her, complete with splendid fireworks.

With the sky illuminated, Marisha swam closer. She caught the Princess's eye.

"Hi, I'm Princess Melody," the land Princess said, crouching on the deck to shake Marisha's hand. "Today is my birthday, would you like to come aboard and join us?"

Marisha was caught off guard. She didn't expect such friendliness. From everything her father had suggested, she expected to be turned away. "I'm Marisha," she replied. "I'm sorry to interrupt your festivities. I'm a mer-person, I've never seen anything like this."

"Well come aboard," Melody said.

"I wish I could, but I don't have legs," Marisha blushed.

"Hmm, that does pose a problem. I'll be right back." Melody zipped off to grab a cushion to sit on, and parked herself beside Marisha so the two could chat.

Melody shared all about her birthday traditions, her family, life at sea, and Marisha did the same. The two split a piece of birthday cake – Marisha had never tasted anything so lovely. Melody told her about the parts of the ship and they had a good laugh about the term 'Poop Deck'.

Unfortunately, while Marisha was getting to know Melody, her absence from the sea kingdom had been noted. When the Sea King discovered that Marisha had gone to the surface, he was livid. He stirred the seas with a terrible storm that soon arrived at Princess Melody's ship.

The skies darkened, waves pitched the party ship, and rain hammered the deck. The party goers ran to protect the ship from damage and Melody sprang into action alongside her crew.

Marisha realised at once what had happened. She plunged back into the sea, hoping to stop her father. But as she swam below she could see the ship was in grave danger, tossing and heaving, creaking and cracking. Instead of continuing to the sea kingdom, Marisha hastened back to the surface to check on her fellow princess.

While the other land-dwellers filled a life boat, Marisha noticed Melody out of reach, clinging to a broken bit of deck that had split off her beloved ship, in desperate need of help. Marisha raced to the rescue and towed Melody to shore just as the ship sank dramatically into the water. Once on dry land, Marisha helped Melody recover. Wringing out her hair, bringing seaweed snacks to restore her energy and keeping her company till the search party arrived. Melody even snoozed on Marisha's shoulder.

When Melody stirred, Marisha had a million questions about life on land. It turned out Melody had just as many about life under the sea. They soon discovered they both had trouble getting through to their parents. Melody longed to explore and travel. She wished to catalogue sea life and preserve its habitats, but her parents brushed off her interests as hobbies. Marisha spoke about the litter that plagued the sea and her ideas to address them. The two princesses' visions lined up perfectly.

When the search party arrived, the princesses said goodbye. They planned to meet again but it would take some creativity and some help.

Upon returning to the sea, Marisha was in big trouble. Because she broke the Sea King's rules she was grounded at her grandmother's place.

Marisha told her grandmother all about her visit to the surface. Her grandmother had an idea and took Marisha to see the sea sorceress, Anteia, who lived where the water

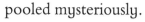

pooled mysteriously.

Marisha was nervous. The sorceress Anteia was welcoming, but peculiar. She explained that there was old magic that could conjure up legs for Marisha, or permit her a few days as a human. Unfortunately, these spells required great sacrifice, like the loss of one's voice or life trapped as a barnacle. That would not do at all.

Instead, the three put their heads together and came up with an inspired invention. Marisha brought her collection of above world debris, and Anteia used her magic to form it all into an open-air Aquarium Rover. This allowed Marisha to keep her tail submerged while travelling in the human world.

As soon as the finishing touches were put on the special vehicle, and the Sea King was away visiting another kingdom, up Marisha went. She found her way to Melody's kingdom, a great island palace beside a strange factory. Melody came out at once and greeted her friend. Marisha turned the Aquarium Rover into 'land' mode and drove up onto the island to meet her. There, Melody gave Marisha a tour of the grounds and palace. When they arrived at the factory, Marisha began to put the pieces together. The factory made wonderful goods that kept the palace in business, but let off litter into the sea.

"I wonder," ventured Melody, "if we used the same methods that built your Aquarium Rover, perhaps we could make a similar kind of container to collect the litter. Then we could get rid of it properly."

"That's a great idea!" said Marisha.

Meanwhile, word of Marisha's cool Aquarium Rover got around. So cool, right? Well the Sea King didn't think so. He overheard some mermaids talking of it in the kingdom he was visiting, and he was furious! At just the moment the princesses were looking at the factory, the Sea King rose to the surface. Seeing the two princesses together, he flew into a rage. He summoned a storm so fierce the sky crackled with lightning, and huge waves crashed down on the shore, putting both princesses in peril. In all the fury, the factory was struck by lightning and a river of litter began to flow out towards the Sea King.

Melody was a skilled sailor. She jumped in the aquarium, clothes and all, and quickly steered the Rover to create a barrier between the Sea King and the factory. As litter streamed out,

Melody spotted a net amongst the debris and grabbed a hold of it. Marisha jumped in after her and the two stretched out the net to stop the flow of litter into the ocean.

As the Sea King watched the two princesses work together, he paused. The storm subsided. He saw their selflessness, their shared mission and their compassion for one another's worlds, and he began to cry happy tears. As his tears hit the water, they brought to the surface all the debris and waste that had sunk over the years. He called upon the sorceress Anteia and together they fashioned all the old junk into a special barge that would take all the waste from the factory and recycle it into usable items.

From that day forward the two kingdoms were bonded together. The princesses lived side by side, with Marisha beneath the surface in an undersea addition to the island palace. Melody had Anteia fashion a special dive suit so she could hang out with her sweetie below the tides.

Over the years, Melody took on oversight of the factory's clean water project, while Marisha focused her energy on brokering lasting peace between the mer-people and the earth dwellers. For this bold work, Marisha received the Fairyland Prize for Peace. Together with her father the Sea King, she regularly visited schools to speak about overcoming prejudice.

The princesses shared not only a vision for the future of their kingdoms, but also a vision for their lives together. Once the waters were clear again, the two were married in a lively and loving ceremony, in a lagoon where both mer-people and humans could enjoy the merriment. Afterwards, the sky was painted with magnificent fireworks – a joint gift from the two kingdoms to the newlyweds.

Rapunzel

Once upon a time, there lived a couple who were expecting a child. As is sometimes the case, the pregnant mother had an appetite for strange new things. The couple forever made extra trips to the market for melon with fennel and sausages with frosting. Her favourite was rapunzel, field greens, which she liked to mix with whipped cheese. When winter rolled around and field greens were out of season, the expectant mother grew desperate. "Oh, dear," she said one day, "if I don't get some rapunzel I don't think the baby and I are going to make it!"

But the couple were in luck, for next door lived a kooky sorceress named Gothel. She was often in a sour mood and so they weren't on the greatest of terms, but being a sorceress, Gothel had an enchanted garden. And within the garden grew rapunzel.

In a moment of desperation, the couple climbed the wall after dark into Gothel's garden. They stole the rapunzel greens so that the mother and baby could allay their cravings. But the following night, when the couple heaved themselves over the wall again, they came face-to-face with Gothel.

"Well, well, what do we have here?" the offended sorceress said. "You're worse than the animals! How could you climb into my garden like a thief and steal my favourite veggies? You owe me for this."

"Oh," the mother answered, "please, it's only because I fear for my well-being and that of my child. I can't find these greens anywhere else and I crave them so badly!"

Gothel's mood softened, and she said, "If things are as dire as you say, I will allow you to take as much rapunzel as you want from my garden."

The couple breathed a sigh of relief.

"But under one condition: you must allow the child that you bring into the world to be my apprentice. They will have magical powers from the garden and will need someone to teach them how to harness them," the sorceress explained.

The couple conferred and agreed it was the only way for everyone to stay healthy and happy. "Plus," the mother said hopefully, "maybe it will improve our relationship as neighbours?"

When the baby arrived, it was a smart and active little girl with hair to spare. The couple named her Rapunzel after the field greens that sustained her. Rapunzel grew up a child of the garden. She ran free, let her long hair down and built archways with twigs and limbs to play beneath. When winter weather brought Rapunzel indoors

she would pass the time braiding her hair and stacking things. She stacked boxes, cushions, jars and cups, to make towers and pillars. Her parents noted her interest in building and felled a tree to make her wooden building blocks.

When Rapunzel came of age, the family – as promised – sent their daughter next door to study under the guidance of the sorceress Gothel. Rapunzel's studies were to take place far away in a tall tower that stood in a lush forest. It was the custom that pupils of magic study in isolation until their powers were well mastered, for fear of magical blunders that could put others in danger. The tower Gothel selected was made from rare stone but the builders had run out of material before they could finish. It lacked a door and a stairway, and had only a tiny little window at the very top.

To get in, Rapunzel had to scale the stony exterior. Since she had splendid long hair, once atop the tower she pulled her hair into a band and then let her long ponytail fall to the ground so the sorceress could climb up, too.

This elaborate system meant that Rapunzel and the sorceress only went out one at a time, and the sorceress, as the teacher, took priority. When she wanted to enter, she simply stood below and called out:

"Rapunzel, Rapunzel, let down your hair!"

And Rapunzel would let her hair fall down like a great rope. It wasn't an ideal system, but it worked okay at first.

In the tower, Gothel introduced Rapunzel to the mysteries of sorcery. Together they tried to identify what effect the enchanted greens may have had on Rapunzel. The two experimented with shape-shifting, but Rapunzel remained herself, just a bit stiff. They tried their hands at healing, but Rapunzel just ended up with a bad case of food poisoning.

"Perhaps you can conjure animals?" mused Gothel. But instead of beasts, the tower ended up filled with rainbow hard-boiled eggs!

They tried magical skill after magical skill, but nothing worked. One evening over a solemn pot of tea, while Gothel fretted about what to do next, Rapunzel spoke up.

"May I make some improvements around the tower?" she offered. "Maybe if we had more space, it could make things easier for our work? I might even be able to create a space to have company, my parents, or perhaps a magic doctor."

"I don't see why not," sighed the sorceress. "I'm not sure what else to do. Plus, I'm getting a little weary from all the climbing and I'm sure your hair could use a break."

The following day, Rapunzel lowered herself on her own hair and began to circle the tower. She spent the entire day asking Gothel to toss things down to her.

"Can I get a sketch pad of graph paper and a ruler?" Rapunzel called up. "And a level and some string?"

"Goodness, what do you have in mind?" wondered Gothel.

"I'm making a pendulum." Rapunzel replied eagerly. "I could use some chalk if we have it?"

As the sun set, Rapunzel called up to Gothel, "Can you toss down a canvas tarp and a blanket? I think I'll be camping out here. I'm onto something, I just need a little more time."

"Well in that case," Gothel said, "you'll need a warm fire and a basket of supper." And with a visit to her magic cauldron Gothel conjured up a bright warm lamp and basket with a hot meal. She sailed them down to Rapunzel on a parachute made from a cosy blanket.

In the morning, Gothel woke and peered out of the tower window to discover Rapunzel was already up and busy drafting a plan for how to change the tower.

"I think I can add a lift up the side and other attachments to help the space breathe," Rapunzel shouted excitedly.

In the weeks that followed, the two forgot about trying to find Rapunzel's magic gift. Instead, they worked tirelessly. They raised a pulley system and attached a bucket to create a lift. Then they created an extension bridge from the tower to a new platform which was to become the guest room. Rapunzel sourced building materials from the forest and Gothel used her magic to fell trees, mill timber and even draw forth boulders from a nearby river so that they floated like bubbles through the air. When they were finished, the stones formed a massive enchanted escalator, while an adjacent lift ferried groceries and luggage. The fresh timber formed a tree house that joined the tower via a suspension bridge. The top of the tower was elevated to reveal a stained-glass room which let in natural light and along each side of the tower was a trellis, which became a living garden to provide the tower with fresh vegetables and herbs.

As the project neared completion, it happened that a prince was riding through the forest. As he approached the magnificent structure he stopped in his tracks. The Prince was blind, and so he heard the tower first. It sounded incredible! The Prince took in the whirr of bees, the sway and creak of the bridge. He felt the warm reflection the stained glass cast on his skin and asked his horse to lower him to the ground. The Prince stepped off and explored the amazing things that surrounded him. He felt the rope and bucket of the pulley. He rested his hands on the great floating boulders and strolled beneath the shade of the tower.

He rode home, the senses of the stunning tower lingering in his mind. And he returned to the forest every day to listen to the goings-on at the construction site. One time, as he was standing behind a tree, he heard the sorceress approach, and say:

"Rapunzel, Rapunzel, let down your hair!"

Rapunzel let down her lovely hair, and tied at the bottom was a golden key which clinked along the tower on the way down. The Prince leaned in closer and listened carefully as the sorceress took the key, strode around to the garden trellis, and placed the key in a key hole. With the turn of the key, the orbiting boulders stood to attention, and then in a dance with the breeze, they moved to form a seamless path that the sorceress climbed gently like bouncing stairs. Together Gothel and the boulders rose to the tower door where Rapunzel greeted her. The Prince heard it all.

"That is unlike any tower I've ever heard," he remarked. And the next day, just as it was beginning to get dark, he went to the tower and called:

"Rapunzel, Rapunzel, let down your hair!"

But when the Prince listened for the clink of the key he heard no sound. So, the Prince turned his ear to Rapunzel, who he could

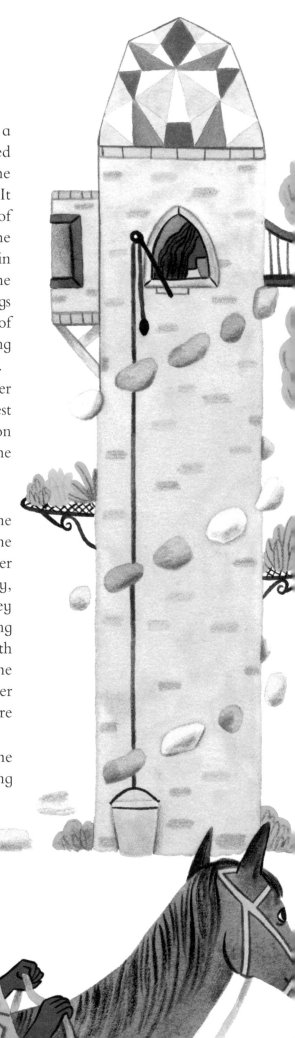

hear striding down the enchanted stone escalator.

"We don't give keys to just anyone," Rapunzel said. "My teacher and mentor Gothel has had some trouble with thieves in the past," she added with a smile.

"Of course, how silly of me," said the Prince. "I'm Prince Eustace, and you are?"

"Oh, I'm Rapunzel, like the vegetable."

"So nice to meet you. I'm so taken with your tower. Did you design it yourself?" the Prince inquired.

"I did. Come on in, I'll give you a tour," said Rapunzel.

"I'd love that!" Eustace beamed. "You may not have noticed, but I'm visually impaired. Do you mind if I take your arm?"

"No problem! We are just days from a ribbon cutting," Rapunzel said, as they ascended with linked elbows.

Gothel joined the two at the tower door and together the three toured the structure.

"I like how you kept the original tower but augmented it to suit your needs," reflected Prince Eustace. "As a person who is blind, there are many buildings in my kingdom that I love but that don't work for me. We could use a mind like yours."

"I'd gladly help you with that," offered Rapunzel. "That's sort of how this project got started, really. We were using the tower to help me find out if I have any magic powers, but we were too cramped."

"Why, it seems obvious to me what your power is," said Eustace.

"What do you mean?" puzzled Gothel and Rapunzel at once.

Prince Eustace had to keep himself from laughing. "You're an exceptional and downright magical architect!" he pronounced.

Gothel and Rapunzel looked around and then at each other. "Of course," said Gothel with a shake of her head. "It's been right in front of us this whole time." Rapunzel went red in the face with pleasure.

Rapunzel turned out to be one of the most creative and unequivocally magical designers and architects of her time. After the ribbon-cutting ceremony at the tower, Rapunzel went to work on royal commissions for Prince Eustace and others. She improved buildings for the blind, planned a flame-retardant village for fire-breathing creatures and re-sized a bridge for trolls. She built some of the most famous constructions in Fairyland, including Aurora's public library, the Snow Queen's winter sports complex and Puss and Boots' animal sanctuary. Her firm, A Braid Above, attracted designers and architects the world over, eager to join Rapunzel in pioneering technologies to enrich places and spaces for all.

Her firm, A Braid Above, attracted architects the world over.

The Snow Queen

Once upon a time, in a mountain region, stood a beautiful palace. In the palace lived a King, Queen and their daughter, Princess Sesi.

Sesi loved to explore the vast landscape of the kingdom. There were great frozen lakes, glacial mountains with waterfalls, snow-laden alpine forests and hidden ice caves glistening with diamond-like icicles. Naturally, she enjoyed many outdoor sports and this early interest set her on a track to become a great athlete.

Sesi's partner in fun was her school companion and neighbour, Alena. Both from snowy mountain kingdoms, the two friends would meet up at the halfway point between their homes. There they practised archery, zipped down alpine slides and raced toboggans, shouting "Yip, zip, skadoooooo!" and spotted one another while mountain climbing. The two friends even had matching scars from slipping on the frozen lake, since neither were very good skaters!

Princess Sesi and Alena went to the same boarding school and would stay up late planning their dream winter play complex.

"Our dream snow park will cover a whole mountainside!" schemed Alena.

"With state of the art toboggans," Sesi announced.

"A full-time trail groomer, so the conditions are always perfect."

"An animal park with a reindeer reserve and a place for owl viewing."

"And a hot chocolate kiosk every mile!" they laughed.

They also loved making up great jokes, like this gem: *Where does a polar bear keep its money? In a snow bank!*

Princess Sesi and Alena thought they'd be best friends forever. Then, one day, Princess Sesi was putting her toboggan away in the palace storeroom when something shiny caught her eye. She followed the glint of light, and found a mirror tucked behind a stack of old paintings and boards. It seemed to draw her in like a magnet.

The mirror was extraordinary. It was big enough to reflect a whole figure. Shiny platinum outlined its face and formed a pattern of decorative snowflakes. Princess Sesi balanced the mirror against her knee and leaned in to examine the astonishing handiwork. But as she did so, she slipped on some black ice on the cold stone

floor and the mirror crashed to the ground, sending shards of glass everywhere like a storm of diamonds. "Phew," said Princess Sesi, for she didn't think she'd been harmed – but a tiny sliver of the mirror had entered her chest and pierced her heart.

From that day on, Princess Sesi was not the same. The splinter in her heart had changed her. The mirror that Sesi found had been created long ago by a cruel troll, who had cast a spell so that anyone who was struck by its glass would see the world through unkind eyes.

Sesi lost her sense of humour and her sense of adventure. She complained about everything from the temperature of food to the softness of linens. She spread her bad mood everywhere she went.

When school commenced, Princess Sesi returned to the suite she lived in with her friend and neighbour, Alena. As room-mates they had shared clothes, stories and even a potted rose bush that they tended in their common room. Their suite was usually the place to be, and other classmates were always stopping by. But with the splinter of glass in her heart, Sesi acted differently.

"We're dressing up today, would you like to wear my tiara?" offered Alena.

"No way, it makes you look like a chandelier. I'd never be seen in that," Sesi snapped.

"I grabbed a milkshake at the canteen," Alena tried later. "Want to split it?"

"Gross, who would want your germs?" was Sesi's retort. "Plus, you know those treats are made with troll slop?"

Alena was confused. What was up with her friend? Alena took to watching her closely. With games Sesi was a grouch, throwing up a board when things weren't going her way. Sesi accused her classmates of cheating if she lost at tests. At art, she coloured on their drawings with her own ink. The nerve! At music, she sang loudly over everyone else.

At sports, Sesi was the nastiest. She was overly competitive and bitter. "Walk it off," she'd yell at injured skiers on the slopes. "Is that the best you can do?" she'd say in the hockey locker room. "You are losers!" Sesi would shout at opposing teams.

"It's as if ice runs in her veins," the other athletes shuddered. Soon, Sesi's mates gave up on her. All except Alena, for she knew that buried deep inside Sesi was a good person, her true friend. When the next school break rolled around and no one wanted to include Sesi, Alena invited her to join her family's dog-sled race.

The race took them on rustic sleds up frozen rivers, through a snow-covered enchanted garden to a cosy lodge. Sesi pranced around like a princess and threw snowballs at the dogs. Everyone rolled their eyes. In the garden, she complained that Alena's family's ice fountains were much smaller than hers. Again, everyone rolled their eyes. Then, as the starting gun sounded, Sesi jumped on the fastest sled

and
sped
off into
the distance.
"Eat my dust!" she
shouted.

Sesi didn't even look back.
If she had, she would have seen
that moments later a band of thieves
descended upon Alena and her family. They
were robbed of everything: snacks, supplies, coats,
dogs – even their boots! As the family gathered themselves,
Alena struggled to stand. She cried out when she tried to walk.
The grown-ups ran for help, leaving Alena alone.

Meanwhile, Princess Sesi pressed on at top speed and arrived gleefully at the finish line. "Yessss!" she roared and went into a showy victory dance. But no one was there to greet her. "Hey, where is everybody? No trumpets, no parade?" she yelled, looking around. "Doesn't anyone want to shake the hand of a winner?"

No celebration commenced, no awards were given out. Instead, a sign on the lodge door read: *Race cancelled due to incident. Beware roving bands of thieves.*

Steaming, Sesi turned to head back. She raced furiously back to the start, hoping to find someone to yell at. Instead, she found Alena collapsed in her path.

"Can you believe this stupid race?!" Sesi complained.

Alena, pale and hurt, with only socks on her feet, tried to answer. But she shook with cold and tears rolled down her cheeks. Something stirred in Sesi's heart. She could see Alena was in real trouble.

Sesi approached her friend, took off her mittens and gently slid them on Alena's frozen feet. The stirring in Sesi's heart grew. She shrugged out of her coat and wrapped it around Alena's shoulders. The colour returned to Alena's face, and with that, the splinter of mirror that had plagued the Princess for so long was released, and Sesi began to glow with warmth.

Sesi sat beside her friend and hugged her to keep her warm. "I'm sorry," she whispered. "I feel like I haven't been myself lately."

"I knew you were in there somewhere," said Alena, snuggling against Sesi's renewed glow.

"Thank you for never giving up on me," Sesi said. "I think I know how I can repair things, if given the chance." Sesi explained to Alena her idea to gift the kingdom with a wonderful wintery playground, just like the one they planned as youngsters.

Alena nodded. "You'll make a great Queen of Winter someday," she smiled, grateful to have her friend back. And as winter thawed around them, the two friends looked towards their bright and sunny future.

When Sesi became Queen, she realised her grand plan and created The Snow Queen Sports Complex. It more than made up for her spell of nastiness. There she coached youngsters on the slopes with a balance of rigour and compassion, and good sportsmanship above all. Sesi's students helped her follow her own coaching rules and became a record-holding athlete herself.

Alena visited every winter to cheer on the ice hockey teams and teach mountaineering first aid. In the evenings, the friends always left time to meet up at one of the dozen hot chocolate kiosks, warm themselves by the fire (with mittens on their feet) and share silly jokes, like:

Knock knock.

Who's there?

Freeze.

Freeze who?

Freeze a jolly good fellow! Freeze a jolly good fellow!

"I knew you were in there somewhere," said Alena.

Elisabeth and the Wild Swans

Once in a small country lived a king and a queen. They had each been married before and together they created a big blended family of twelve children. They tucked themselves snuggly into a modest palace, with the children sharing rooms. Their toys, games and accessories spilled out into the common areas, gardens and grounds. One day, after a visitor tripped on a domino so hard his fake teeth flew out, the royal family built the kids a playhouse in the woods.

There the twelve kids played the days away with imaginative games, gardening, performing and building. During their games, they all learned what they were good at, and what they might become when they grew up. Rodney excelled in circus arts, Maude proved a budding chemist. Jay – an engineer – built a pulley system to bring snacks aboard. Grace raced boats on the pond, Eugenia liked to play doctor with her dolls and Beauregard, an apprenticing electrician, put up lights.

The eldest of the kids, Princess Elisabeth, was a real chatterbox. She was a dabbler and lent a hand with her siblings' interests. But she hadn't yet discovered what really captured her attention.

Nearby the playhouse in the woods, there lived two young wizards, Wess, and his sister Wanda. One day, while Elisabeth was preparing everyone a snack at the playhouse, the youngsters were playing Hot Potato and an errant ball shattered the window of Wess's office. He had been practising a delicate spell that turned a mouse into a swan. But the ball through the window jostled the magic and – with a loud bang and lots of smoke – it flashed through the window and onto the kids! Before the young wizard's eyes the children turned into eleven beautiful swans.

The children, now covered in feathers, flapped about trying their new wings and bumping into one another. Before long, Wess, Wanda, the King, Queen and Princess Elisabeth were all on the scene.

"What's happened?" cried the Queen. "Where are the children?"

The King went white, gazing at the swans. "I think we're looking at them."

"I'm so sorry!" cried the wizard, embarrassed. "I'm sure I can fix it."

The poor wizard tried desperately to alter the spell, but to no avail. The swans kept on strutting and squawking about.

"There must be a spell to reverse it in your books," Elisabeth said, heading to the wizard's office. Wanda joined Elisabeth and consulted the wizardly texts. Soon enough they located a passage and Wanda read it aloud for everyone to hear.

"The transfiguration of swans: impacts include flying all day, resting only by night.

Before the young wizard's eyes the children turned into eleven beautiful swans.

Side effects include squawking, wing rash and webbed feet. Spell may be reversed by the donning of a hand-knit nettle shirt—"

"Fantastic!" cried the King.

"Wait, there's more," continued Wanda. "The shirt must be knitted by an immediate relative who may not speak a word the entire time. Shirts must be knitted in two months' time, or—"

"Or the person must stay a swan forever!" Elisabeth read over Wanda's shoulder.

The King gulped. "It's hopeless. Where are we going to find a relative who is a master seamstress who could work that fast, and doesn't mind being stung by nettles?!"

Princess Elisabeth spoke up. "I could do it."

"No way," said the King.

"But I'm good with my hands, and I'm a quick learner," said the Princess. "Please, let me do this. I'd never forgive myself if my brothers and sisters were swans forever!"

The King and Queen conferred and agreed that Princess Elisabeth would move into the playhouse in the woods, where she could collect nettles and set to work.

That very afternoon, Elisabeth began collecting nettles that grew on the floor of the woods. They nipped and burned and left red blotches on her hands, but Wanda showed her where to find some soothing berries. These helped and soon Elisabeth had enough nettles to get started. Wincing, she stepped on the nettles to break them down, then twisted the fibres to spin them into coarse thread.

Making the first shirt was a little clumsy but Elisabeth persisted. She traced her own clothing and looked for the places where different pieces of fabric joined together. After a few days, it was complete. Its neckline was maybe too deep and one sleeve was longer than the other, but it was a success nonetheless.

For the next shirt, Elisabeth planned more carefully. She folded her pattern to be sure it was symmetrical and she noticed some seeds in Wanda and Wess' yard that she added as buttons. With each shirt Elisabeth learned something new. For the third shirt Wanda showed Elisabeth how to make vegetable dyes to colour it red. For the fourth, Wess turned the shattered window into glitter, which Elisabeth dusted on the seams. On the fifth, Elisabeth tried a fancy collar, and on the sixth shirt, bark buckles. With each one, the Princess thought of a specific brother or sister – what they might like if they were human again. And on each one she embroidered a tiny winged motif.

After a month had passed, Elisabeth ventured into the woods to forage for nettles and discovered she'd used them all up! Her heart pounding in panic, she pressed on until she arrived at a great walled garden. Peeking over the hedge she saw that it was full of wildflowers, herbs, veggies and… nettles!

"Score!" Elisabeth thought in her head, since of course she could not speak out loud. She had no way to ask permission, so she shimmied through the hedge and into the garden.

Immediately Elisabeth began collecting the nettles and stuffing them in her pinafore, her stockings, even under her bonnet. Thinking of her brothers and sisters, and what little time she had left before they'd be swans forever, she collected with such haste and frenzy that dirt and roots flew everywhere.

This attracted the attention of the owners of the garden: another royal family with a young prince named Felix, who happened to be out on a bike. The Prince's companion, the huntsman, mistook Elisabeth's action for the work of a thief. He plucked her from the garden and Elisabeth was soon shut up in a far tower of the castle.

In her lonely room, Elisabeth was in despair. She had neither her needles or her precious nettles. No one knew where she was. A month had already passed, how would she finish the shirts in time? She could not cry out so she went to the window and looked to the horizon.

All at once, as if by magic, a flock of swans graced the sky. Princess Elisabeth waved to them and they drew closer. As the birds came towards her, Elisabeth could see that in their feet they held a great net. And in the net, was a supply of nettles, flowers, nuts and seeds, plus coloured dyes in jars and berries.

Elisabeth jumped for joy, and as the swans hovered outside the tower window, she collected all the items from the net. For the next few

weeks, Elisabeth stayed in the tower and worked as fast as she possibly could, until it was the final day of the two month deadline.

Prince Felix was intrigued by the silent guest. He didn't think she was a thief. But when he knocked on the door, Elisabeth turned him away.

Prince Felix tried being funny. "Cat got your tongue?" Elisabeth made a face.

Then he tried to be serious. "My family want to put you on trial today and lock you up for quite some time. What were you doing in the garden?"

Elisabeth opened the door and Felix was greeted with piles and piles of nettle yarn coiled in the corner. Jars of dye and seeds and berries littered the floor.

"What is all of this?" he tried again gently.

Elisabeth just shook her head and went back to her work. She knew there was only one afternoon remaining before her siblings would be left as swans forever! She still had a final shirt to make, and didn't know how she would finish in time.

When Felix saw her eagerly working away, despite the pain in her hands, he realised she must be doing something really important. He only had one more question. "How about I help you?" Felix said, settling in on the floor.

Elisabeth nodded exuberantly. Some hours later, they had just finished the final shirt when the sun was setting, and keys jangled in the door. It was the huntsman, who had come to take Elisabeth to her trial.

Eyebrows raised, Felix raced to the door to hold off the huntsman while Elisabeth, shirts in hand, ran to the window and waved frantically.

At just that moment the swans could be seen arriving over the woods. The largest swan spotted Elisabeth in the tower and swooped up to collect her. They flew fast across the treetops and with a rush

of wings, landed as gracefully as snow falling in the garden. The King, Queen, Wess and Wanda burst through the woods to join them.

The King hurriedly dressed swans one and two, the Queen dressed swans three and four, Wess and Wanda dressed swans four, five, six and seven and Elisabeth dressed nine and ten. But when she reached for the final shirt for the eleventh swan, it was not to be found. Panic rose in her face and she looked from family to friends.

All of a sudden, they heard the voice of Felix. "Princess, Princess!" he shouted, "you left something behind!" Prince Felix appeared over the horizon, shirt in hand, and covered with painful prickles.

Princess Elisabeth gratefully accepted the shirt from Felix and slid it over the head of the eleventh swan. With the final shirt on, the whole flock rose in a great whirl of feathers and light, and transformed back into a group of smiling children.

The family rejoiced and admired their new finery. For when the swans took their human form once again, their nettle shirts transformed as well. The eleven children now wore fine garments with jewels where there had been seeds, gold and silver where there had been glitter, each collar delicately embroidered with wings.

"These are beautiful," the children mused, touching their clothes with wonder.

"We've never seen anything like them!" the King and Queen noted.

"I think you've found your calling," predicted Prince Felix.

Princess Elisabeth, who hadn't spoken in months, simply said with a smile, "Why, yes, I think I have."

As the years passed, Princess Elisabeth's reputation and skills grew and grew, until she became one of the most talented and sought-after fashion designers in the realm. When she and her siblings took over the kingdom, she secured its future by making it a centre of clothing design. For years, Princess Elisabeth dressed commoners to VIPs under her very own fashion label, called White Feather.

Cinderella

There was once a kingdom in which lived all manner of people. Royalty, merchants, artisans, performers, chefs, teachers, doctors, scientists and many fine people who hadn't quite figured out what they were yet. One of whom was Ella.

Ella's parents had recently passed away after long illnesses. They had lived noble lives, and so were buried near a steadfast hazel tree. Ella was sad to say goodbye to her parents, but she took a small hazel tree seedling, and set off. It was time for her to find purpose in a new place.

Upon arriving in the city centre, Ella planted her hazel tree, then sought work. At home, she had been excellent at organising, and kept everything tidy and clean for her folks in their last days. So when she noticed an advertisement in the town square for a house cleaner, she donned her overalls, and off she went to the address listed in the advert.

The family, a woman and her two daughters, hired her on the spot. Each day, Ella cleaned floors, dusted surfaces, wiped glass and tidied steps. The woman and her daughters were terribly demanding. They were always coming up with extra jobs, from fixing squeaky doors to assembling furniture, organising closets to gluing together broken dishes (which Ella was sure they broke on purpose). It would have been bearable if they paid her a living wage, but when they remembered to pay her – which wasn't often – it was just pennies. On top of that, they bullied Ella with cruel names and nasty pranks, writing mean messages on the mirrors.

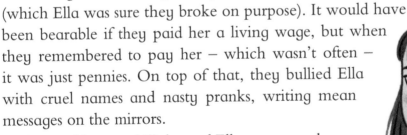

"Enough's enough!" shouted Ella on one such an instance. And with that, she handed in her notice.

Ella didn't want to have another bad employer, so she decided to go into business for herself. She was careful to only take on clients who paid fairly and offered respectful working conditions. Her hard work paid off and soon her small business of one grew to include a few employees. Ella discovered that people who are treated better work better and soon she and her team found themselves in high demand.

They cleaned up after chimney sweeps a lot, so they decided to offer the service themselves. The scheme worked so well that soon the company became known as Cinder-Ella's.

Through her classes and her colleagues, Ella met many wonderful people that worked in homes, gardens and castles, helping the kingdom run smoothly. Her new friends worked in back kitchens and cellars, plodded up steep stairs, hung from tower windows and toiled in hot gardens. They shared their experiences with Ella, the hardships and the rewards. But Ella noticed that she and her friends, despite their hard work, were not making enough to grow their businesses or have homes of their own.

So Ella began organising her friends to attend local meetings and share their stories. She created a small business association and wrote letters to the leaders of the land (like MPs), offering a glimpse into the life of those in service, and suggestions for ways to make the kingdom a more just and equal place to live. One day she even wrote to the King!

The King had no idea of the plight of those who toiled in the kingdom, and was surprised and shaken by Ella's cause. He announced he would hold a benefit ball to support efforts to make their lives better.

Ella was thrilled. She hadn't even expected a reply and now the King was going to be an advocate! And she was excited to attend the royal ball. There was just one hitch: Ella's wardrobe consisted of only work clothes. Tattered overalls, grimy shirts, work boots. These weren't really ball options. All the money Ella made at work went into the business, so she had nothing extra to spend on party attire or hiring a carriage. She was in a real pickle. And when Ella found herself in a pickle, she often found her way to the small hazel tree she had brought with her. Sitting beneath it, she wondered aloud, "How am I ever going to get to this ball? I've nothing to wear, no carriage to take me…"

As if to answer her query, a brisk breeze swept through the garden, and blew the leaves about, setting a magical moment in motion. For as the leaves settled, a most unusual lady was revealed. She had a wild head of hair, several pairs of spectacles, and a glittering wand in her hand.

"Do I know you?" asked Ella, amazed.

"Oh, I'm your Fairy Godmother of course," said the mysterious guest. "Does that ring a bell? I've been watching you for a while now, dear Ella, and you've been doing so incredibly well for yourself.

I was beginning to wonder if you'd ever need me. There's really nothing you can't do, my dear," she continued, "except perhaps fix your closet crisis. Would you like my help?"

"A real Fairy Godmother, eh?" Ella said, collecting herself. "I'm stunned. But if your offer really stands, then yes. I would love your help with something to wear to the ball. I think this could be a big night for me, and I want to feel great. You know what I mean?"

"I think I do," said her Fairy Godmother with a twinkle in her eye. "First, a carriage!" And with a wave of her wand an antique coach rolled gently before them.

"Oh, my!" gasped Ella.

"And for you to wear, my dear," her Fairy Godmother put her arm around Ella, "I've something special in store."

As Ella's Fairy Godmother withdrew her arm from her shoulder, lovely leaves and aromatic hazelnuts whirred around them both and came to a stop in the shape of a green crown that landed gently on Ella's head. Meanwhile, a spring-green dress of Ella's dream length and cut draped her in the softest and lightest of fit.

"Oh, this is amazing!" Ella cried. "And I know just what to pair it with."

"You mean you don't want any fancy shoes?" invited her Fairy Godmother.

"Oh, no I've just the thing," Ella called back as she darted towards her house.

Ella raced to her closet and topped the whole look off with her favourite emerald-green shoes. They were perfect for all occasions, plus she'd never seen anyone else in them, ever.

"Now zip along, you've a ball to enjoy," said her Fairy Godmother, hurrying her into the carriage. "And please return everything you borrowed back here to the hazel tree at the end of the night. The tree will be missing its leaves."

Ella arrived at the ball looking and feeling brilliant. The music was amazing, everything smelled delicious and there was dancing! While her friends set off to mingle, Ella sought out the King to discuss her cause. There turned out to be quite a queue, and as Ella waited she felt a tap on her shoulder.

"Amazing shoes, Princess," said an unfamiliar voice.

Ella spun around to come face to face with someone new, a prince in fact, but Ella didn't notice. She was too distracted by the fact that he was wearing her exact same, one-of-a-kind (or so she thought) shoes. But his were blue!

"Amazing shoes, yourself," Ella finally stammered.

"I'm Prens," said the Prince. "I see we have similar tastes. How'd you like to try on the blue version?" Prens slipped out of one of his shoes and handed it to Ella.

"Are you serious? Absolutely!" Ella slipped out of one of her green shoes and

"I know just what to pair this with," said Ella.

reached for Prens' blue version, which looked simply super.

Prens and Ella chatted the night away while they waited in line for the King. They sang along to the popular songs of the day, shared their interests and even spoke about matters bigger than themselves, which touched whole kingdoms.

"I'm visiting from a small, far-off land, and I'm very interested in your kingdom's commitment to care for its workers," Prens explained. "I heard it all started with a letter from a local. Can you believe it? I'd love to pick that person's brain."

"Oh, well I can tell you some neat facts about that if you like," Ella said excitedly. But at just that moment her name was called for her audience with the King, and she was pulled from the line in haste.

"We'll catch up after!" she called to her new friend as she raced off.

"Wait, I didn't get your name!" Prens called after her. "And I have your shoe."

But Ella was long gone into the depths of the castle. After a successful conversation with the King, she had just left his chamber when she heard the clock strike midnight.

"Oh, no!" she thought to herself. "The hazel tree will be missing its leaves."

With a last look for her shoe doppelganger, she left the ball. "What a shame," she lamented, once she was safely in the carriage. "It's so rare I meet someone with whom I'm so in sync."

The days passed, and time marched on. The success of the King's benefit ball was felt throughout the kingdom. New laws were introduced that let small businesses flourish. Working conditions improved and new houses were built.

However, Ella felt lonely for someone to celebrate these great milestones with. She wished she knew how to reach Prens – her new friend and sole-mate.

Meanwhile, Prens in his kingdom was feeling the same. He was on the cusp of making positive change in his small corner of the world, yet was missing a partner he could learn from and share the success with. He thought he might have had a glimpse of such a person when he met his amazing shoe twin at the benefit ball. But sadly, he didn't know her name nor where to find her.

Rather than sit around and pout, Prens saddled up his horse and started to ask around. The good news was he still had Ella's unique green shoe to help guide the way.

And guide the way it did. For everywhere Prens visited, he was told, "No one here has a shoe quite like that, but I've heard of a great woman doing the work you speak of in a kingdom not far from here."

Slowly but surely, Prens made his way to the great kingdom where Ella was busy leading the Business Affairs Council, unifying workers and seeking fairness wherever she saw that things were unjust. And of course, wearing amazing mismatched shoes.

One day after a particularly prickly town meeting (things don't always go smoothly, even in fairytale kingdoms) Ella walked home exhausted. As she turned in her gate something under the hazel tree caught her eye. It was her green shoe!

"Prens?! Is that you?" Ella called out.

"It is indeed," he said as he rose from behind the tree. "Our shoes are finally reunited!"

"Is that why you came to find me?" asked Ella.

"Well, it's not the only reason," Prens said. "I think we have much more to talk about, more songs to sing along to and more parties to enjoy. I had to find you."

"I'm so glad you did," Ella cheered.

"It would have been a lot easier if I'd known your name," Prens laughed.

"It's Ella," she said. "My friends call me Cinderella. There's a story."

Prens and Ella spent every day together after that. Working together, getting to know one another's friends and kingdoms, sitting under the hazel tree together and, of course, sharing shoes.

When Prens and Ella eventually married, they moved to a new kingdom where a leader such as Ella was so needed. There, she became Prime Minister and worked tirelessly to raise the minimum wage so that all members of the kingdom could prosper. Her constituents too called her Cinderella, to honour her first business. It was the start of a life in leadership, service and seeking justice for all.

The Goose Girl

There once lived a queen who had been a widow for many years. Her late husband, the King, had been a gifted musician and started a summer camp for kids interested in the performing arts. The King and Queen had a daughter, Princess Liesel. When she was old enough, she was enrolled at the summer camp to follow in the footsteps of her father and study music. The only problem was, Liesel could barely carry a tune!

Nearby in the village was a talented youngster, the Baker's daughter, Greta. She loved to sing, but only to herself in the bakery as she was a bit shy. Her family thought performing might help her come out of her shell, so they enrolled her in the same summer camp, to study theatre.

The camp was a distant place, and campers had to ride a funicular up a steep mountain through dense fog to reach it. It was a tricky journey and many parents sent good luck charms with their child to keep them safe. The Queen sent Princess Liesel with a special handkerchief embroidered with three red hearts to bring her good luck. Each camper also brought a horse for the journey. Greta had a pony named Gustav. The Princess, on the other hand, had a horse named Falada. And being a royal steed, Falada possessed a special gift – he could speak!

Princess Liesel and Greta were both on the same mountain funicular and nervously made their way to the carriage. They tucked their horses in the back and sat together in the front. After they had ridden for a while, tears began to fall from Greta's eyes.

"Are you okay?" asked Princess Liesel.

"I'm scared," gulped Greta. "I'm not ready for camp. I have such stage fright."

Princess Liesel looked out at the mountains and wondered what she could do to help. "I'm doing the music camp. I think it's kind of different, though. Since I sing like a seal they may just hide me in a choir," she said. "I can see how performing on your own might seem scary at first, but it could be fun in the end! Maybe you could just imagine yourself being good at it? Kind of fake it till you make it?"

"I don't think I could do that," Greta sniffled. "If I can't convince myself, how am I going to convince an audience? I should just go home!"

"You could take my place, almost anyone would be better at music than me," joked Liesel. She took out her special handkerchief and offered it to Greta, who dried her tears as they continued up the mountain.

"Are you serious?" Greta asked cautiously as she blew her nose.

"Well. . . how are you at music?" Liesel ventured.

"I'm okay," admitted Greta. "I sing a little in the bakery back home."

As the funicular approached the top of the mountain the fog melted away and a beautiful camp was revealed.

"Let's do it. I've always wanted to try theatre," Liesel proposed.

When Liesel disembarked and went to mount her horse, the one that was called Falada, Greta stopped her. "Wait, if I'm to be you, I should take your horse and you take my Gustav."

"Oh, right! Good catch," Liesel said with a grin.

They switched jackets, too. Liesel wore Greta's anorak that smelled of yeasted dough and sweets. And Greta took Liesel's golden cape with her family crest on it.

"Who are you?" came a voice from the horse Greta sat upon.

"Oh, my goodness, you talk?" cried Greta, nearly slipping from Falada's saddle.

"Why, of course I talk – I'm royalty. I don't know who you are, though. My owner is Princess Liesel." Falada shook his glorious mane.

"I'm Greta. Liesel was kind enough to switch places with me because I'm so afraid to go on stage," Greta explained. "You won't spoil our plan, will you?"

"Humph. I'm here for the royal treatment. You'll have to straighten up a bit and ride in there with your head held high! I'll not be slighted my regal rights," Falada grumped.

And so, Greta straightened her posture, took a deep breath and rode into camp.

Upon arrival, there was great celebrating of the campers. There were name games, bunk assignments and a big bonfire to make the first night special. The two girls scarcely crossed paths. Liesel was led straight to the amphitheatre and Greta to the music room. The swapping worked out alright that first day. Greta felt less nervous and Liesel was downright bubbly about theatre. But it wasn't without its glitches.

Greta kept forgetting to answer to her borrowed name. "Liesel? Liesel? Princess?" her counsellor asked as she stood idle beside her. And it took time for Greta to get used to everyone smiling at her, curtseying and giving her knowing looks.

Liesel, on the other hand, noticed that no one treated her as royalty. She was the same as everyone else. She found it a great relief. One new thing for Liesel was farm work. Greta had signed up for a job to help pay for camp and had been paired with a work buddy named Conrad. Together they were expected to tend to the geese that were part of the camp's farm.

Liesel didn't have much experience with farm work, much less fowl. "You move like a bird yourself," Conrad jested as Liesel skittered after the geese. When she held her nose to scrape poo off her shoe, she slipped and fell in the mud. "Steady there," Conrad said, with brows raised and an outstretched hand.

Early one morning, when Princess Liesel and Conrad drove the flock out to the pasture, Falada was out grazing in it. Seeing Princess Liesel looking after the geese, he kicked the dirt with his hoofs and hissed, "Princessssss."

"Did you say something?" Conrad asked, hearing the voice.

The Princess gave Falada a warning look, but he replied:

"Alas, young queen, passing by,

If this your father knew,

He'd not be delighted for you."

"Was that you?" asked Conrad, looking around for the source of the voice.

"Oh, why it's just me pretending to be. . . the horse, of course." Liesel tried to turn her panic into a joke.

The two drove the geese into the field and stopped to rest on a log. Liesel took the break to braid her hair.

"Your hair looks so fancy, could you do mine that way, too?" Conrad asked. "I only wear this tired bun."

Liesel positioned herself above his head, but at just that moment Falada rode by and opened his big, grumpy mouth.

"Blow, blow, blow wind, blow,

Take Conrad's hair, and tie it up so."

After his words, a strong wind came up and blew Conrad's hair into a plait.

"How'd you do that?" Conrad jumped to his feet and marvelled.

Liesel was speechless.

"You have to use that funny

voice in our acting class this afternoon. You're a natural with voices!"

Liesel gulped. It seemed she would have to come up with some funny impressions, or she and Greta's secret swap would be discovered.

Later on, at the music gazebo it was time for the real Greta's first singing lesson. She was so nervous she could scarcely get off a note. Behind her a couple of campers were talking about a girl who does a horse impression.

"It's amazing, she brays and stamps her feet and everything," one kid said to the other.

"I hear she might even have magical powers," the other kid added.

They erupted with giggles. The giggles were contagious, and Greta giggled too, which helped her to relax.

Greta went on to have a great first lesson, singing louder and prouder than she knew she could. And as weeks passed both friends improved and grew in their craft.

As camp neared its end, the cast was announced for the final showcase. Liesel was cast as the lead in a production about a singing unicorn. Since her singing voice wasn't her greatest asset, a vocalist was paired with her for the songs. Much to her surprise, Greta was cast as the singing voice of Liesel's unicorn.

It was nearly a perfect fit, except for one thing. This was a performance for the parents and that included the Queen, who expected to see Princess Liesel in the orchestra, and the Baker, who expected to see Greta on stage as an actor.

The two girls should have been elated, but instead they were petrified – worried their swap was for nothing. That night, they met in the goose field, in the shadow of grouchy Falada who sulked nearby.

"Everyone will discover our secret swap," fretted Greta.

"Our parents will be so disappointed," lamented Liesel. "I'll disgrace my father's legacy." A tear rolled down her face.

"I'm sorry, this is all my fault," sighed Greta. From her pocket she drew the handkerchief with three hearts Liesel had offered her when she was sad.

Liesel was comforted by the sight of the handkerchief with the hearts. She dried her eyes. "I think it was worth it. I love the stage. I've been coming up with so many funny voices and impressions. I had to, or Falada would have spoilt our secret."

"My singing has been going really well," Greta pepped up.

The two of them were quiet, pondering their new talents, until Falada's snort broke the silence. He'd quietly snuck up and was moved by what he'd heard.

"Blow, blow, blow wind, blow," he said. "Take our troubles and fix it so our unicorn can star in the show."

Once again, the wind swept up just as it had with Conrad's hair, but this time it swept Falada's saddle blanket up and over the girls' heads. The wind lifted them gently from the ground and magically landed them on their feet, side by side, beneath the blanket.

"What was that?" asked a shocked Greta.

"I don't know, it happens sometimes when Falada talks," Liesel confessed.

The horse brayed, "Meet your new costume for the showcase!"

"Only if we're playing two potatoes in a sack," Liesel observed.

"No, I get it!" Greta exclaimed. "We'd share two parts of the same costume!"

"Oh, I see. I could be right beside you doing my funny voice, and you could sing. Falada, you're the best!" Liesel hugged her horse.

On the day of the performance the camp was abuzz and Liesel and Greta were positively giddy. Throughout the show, the two friends moved as one beneath the unicorn costume. Greta sang beautifully, and Liesel brought the character to life with her funny voices.

At the final bow, the two flung their costume up over their heads and the audience erupted with cheers. The Queen's jaw dropped as Liesel was revealed as the unicorn voice. The Baker nearly fell out of her chair at discovering Greta was the beautiful singing voice.

Everyone celebrated with a picnic and the girls visited with their families. "Who knew you were an actress!" the Queen exclaimed. "Your father would be so proud."

"You're not mad?" Liesel asked.

"Oh, never, as long as you're happy," the Queen said.

"Greta, it was a delight to hear you sing in public. I'm so proud of you," the Baker beamed. Greta grinned.

And from that day forward, the two friends shared many summers together at camp, together with their friends including Conrad. They performed duets and coached younger campers as counsellors.

As the years passed, Greta went on to take over the family bakery. When summer came, she closed it for the season to run the summer camp. As Camp Director she instituted a special week called Switcheroo, dedicated to campers finding a friend to switch spots with to see where their talents take them. And of course, Greta started each day with a song.

Liesel went on to become an award-winning actress known for her comedy. She held the record for number of sold-out performances in Fairyland. Her fans called her the Princess of Wit and she drew huge crowds wherever the wind would take her. She lifted spirits, made people laugh, and often performed alongside her silly horse Falada.

*At the final bow, the two flung their costume up over
their heads and the audience erupted with cheers.*

Star and the Twelve Dancers

Once upon a time, there lived a king who was devoted to his twelve incredible children. The princes and princesses kept him wonderfully busy. But as they grew older the King was faced with a mystery.

Each morning, when he opened the bed chamber doors to rouse his children, he was met with a perplexing sight. The floor was strewn with dance shoes of all kinds: ballet slippers, pointe shoes, tap shoes, sticky socks, clogs, shoes with bells, heels and trainers. Sweaty dance clothes rested in piles on the floor and the dustbin overflowed with bandage wrappers and dripping ice packs melting in the morning sun. On top of the mess, the children looked more tired than they had at bedtime. Waking them up for the day was difficult and keeping them awake throughout meals, studies and social occasions proved impossible.

As the children approached adulthood the situation only got worse, so the King published an announcement. He offered a generous prize to anyone who could discover what was keeping his children from sleep at night.

Many different people responded – detectives and fortune tellers, doctors and nurses, astrologers, fairy godmothers and wizards, but no one could solve the mystery. Each stayed the night outside the royal bedroom, drunk a cup of bedtime punch, and in the morning awoke, yawning, unable to say what had happened during the night. The King was left deeply disappointed and worried about his children. How could they reach their full potential if they were so tired all the time?

One day, a man named Enrico saw the poster advertising the award. Enrico was down on his luck. He used to work as a ballet master for a small seaside dance troupe and had nursed great hopes of discovering a fleet of promising dancers, but the truth was he just couldn't find any new talent. Soon, the ballet had closed. Saddened by the loss of his job and dreams, Enrico decided to try his luck at the palace.

On his way, Enrico passed a roadside peddler preparing to close for the day. On the table next to them lay a lonely looking cloak. Enrico felt sorry for the peddler and made an offer of a few pieces of silver for the cloak.

The peddler straightened to reveal a regal person of many seasons with a sprinkling of glitter where their hair should have been.

"Thank you, traveller. I should like that very much," they replied.

"No need to wrap it. I can just wear it," Enrico said with a smile.

The peddler laughed. "I don't know if you'd want to do that. This cloak is special, it will make you invisible."

Enrico's eyes widened. "Well, that could come in handy. I am on my way to solve the mystery of the twelve tired princes and princesses."

"I'll send you on with a word of wisdom then," regarded the peddler. "Don't drink the punch!"

Enrico smiled and set off on his way.

Upon arriving at the castle, Enrico was given a warm welcome with dinner and a roaring fire. Afterwards, he was led to his chambers next door to the princes and princesses, to greet them before bedtime.

First came Pepper, Clove, Ginger and Chive. They were followed by Cassia, Basil, Dill and Rosemary. Then it was Cori-Ander, Fennel and Nigella. Last came Star Anise.

"Uh," Star said, "before we turn in, we'll all have some punch. Cheers to a good night's rest," Star placed the cup at the threshold.

"I don't. . ." Enrico started, but Star had already closed the door that divided the two bedchambers. Enrico thought he could hear giggling from the princes and princesses on the other side.

Enrico retrieved the cup from the floor and swirled it around. He often had a drink of warm milk before bed and went to send the punch down the hatch. But then the words of the peddler came to him: "Don't drink the punch."

Enrico looked around the room for a sink or a basin, but all he saw was a small potted plant. He poured the contents of the cup into the plant, and as he did so, Enrico thought he heard music and bells coming from the princes and princesses' chamber.

Enrico raced to the door and peered through the key hole. What he saw on the other side took his breath away.

A panel in the centre of the floor had been taken up to reveal a downward flight of gleaming silver stairs. The princes and princesses were lined up at the top and had started to parade down them. Each was dressed for dancing. Some in specialised shoes, some in bare feet, some in leather slippers and others in heeled shoes of all styles. One pair of shoes, Ginger's, were wrapped with bells. "That

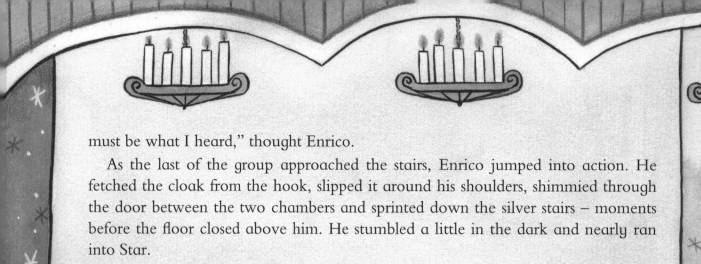

must be what I heard," thought Enrico.

As the last of the group approached the stairs, Enrico jumped into action. He fetched the cloak from the hook, slipped it around his shoulders, shimmied through the door between the two chambers and sprinted down the silver stairs – moments before the floor closed above him. He stumbled a little in the dark and nearly ran into Star.

Feeling a nudge, Star asked in alarm, "Did someone step on my heels?" But the others just rolled their eyes.

As Enrico's eyes adjusted he could see before them a boulevard lined with trees of silver, with shimmering leaves. It was a spectacular sight. The bouncing lantern lights made it look like the inside of a snow globe. As the music grew around him, Enrico went to put a few silver leaves in his pocket, but one slipped through his fingers and dropped to the ground with a clatter. The group turned towards the sound, but Enrico stood perfectly still disguised in his cloak and no one saw a thing.

The music grew louder now and before Enrico's eyes, the silver boulevard pulsed into gold. Gilded birds filled the trees and the path looked as if it was a broad streak of sunset. As they continued, Enrico reached up to touch the branch of a nearby tree. He pulled his hand away and it glittered gold. No one would believe him if he spoke of these marvels, so he snapped off a small branch discreetly.

Soon the group reached a promenade of diamonds, bordering the edge of a lake with a fleet of row boats. Enrico stopped to gape and knelt down to scoop a few stones into his pocket, so when he arrived at the boats they were already filled with the princes and princesses. He jumped into the last boat before it pulled away from shore. It happened to be the boat carrying Star.

"Does the boat feel heavier this evening?" Star asked nervously.

"Oh, it must just be a heavy moon tonight," Chive responded.

Soon the boats came ashore on an island that held a grand pavilion. It shone like a bright star lit with candles. In the centre, a rowdy band played music one couldn't help but dance to. It had a throbbing rhythm like a heartbeat, a bright brass section, a smooth melodic segment and expressive vocals.

Enrico stood on the outskirts of the dance floor and watched, mesmerised, as each of the princes and princesses proved to be a unique and wonderful dancer. Some waltzed, others pranced, a pair glided across the floor like swans. Others drummed their feet and shook their bodies. Some rehearsed set dances while others let the music lead them.

Enrico too swayed to the music and nodded his head with the beat. He closed his eyes and let himself fill with the energy of the room. Enrico was so carried away he dropped his souvenirs, and they fell with a clatter to the floor.

In an instant, the music halted and all eyes fell to the strange pile at Enrico's feet.

"What's that?" questioned Pepper.

"It looks like a collection," said Dill.

"Of stuff from the enchanted path," said Fennel.

"But who would make such a collection?" speculated Cori-Ander.

"A guest, that's who," muttered Pepper.

"Has anyone invited a guest?" asked Clove.

"The mystery solver!" said Ginger.

"You gave him the punch that all our other guests received, didn't you, Star?" Pepper asked, eyes wide.

"I offered the punch, but I can't say I actually saw him drink it," Star confessed.

At that moment Enrico discarded his cloak. Everybody gasped!

"I'm sorry," apologised Enrico. "I only wanted to follow the music. I was in the

ballet you see, and I long for dance."

The siblings looked distraught but Star stepped right up to Enrico and said, "Will you help us conceal our secret?"

Enrico pondered the matter. "I was mesmerised. You all dance so wonderfully. I will help you if you like, but why must you conceal your talents?"

"This world was hidden from us, buried beneath the floor. It's surely forbidden and our father would seal it up if he ever found out," Pepper explained.

"Not if he saw you all dance!" exclaimed Enrico. And with that he gathered his pile of souvenirs and raced back to the palace, the rest of the siblings behind him.

Enrico and the princes and princesses burst though the bed chamber doors just as the sun was rising, waking the King with all the commotion.

"Heavens, what's this? A party at dawn?!" the King shouted.

"Allow me to explain," Enrico began. "Your children are drowsy all day because at night they do not sleep a wink. Instead, they pass beneath their chamber into a magical land paved with silver and gold. They cross a diamond-ringed lake and dance the night away on an island."

The King laughed and laughed. He shook and giggled and slapped his knee. But then Enrico drew forth his hands to reveal the silver leaf, the golden branch and diamonds, and moved so that the King could see the silver steps behind him.

The King quieted and examined the souvenirs with surprise. "Dance you say, what do my children know about dance? We haven't even a ballroom in the castle."

"I think you might need one, Sir. Your children are some of the finest, most innovative and daring dancers I've seen in a great while. Before I had to close my ballet Sir, I dreamed of finding talent such as your children possess."

The King looked to the entire group with awe. And his scepticism turned to pride.

Star stepped forward bravely. "Would you let us dance at home, Father?"

"So long as you always get a good night's sleep," the King grinned.

The King suggested as a reward for Enrico to be the royal ballet master and Enrico was thrilled to support the young dancers. The silver stairs were made permanent and when the children left home, a great theatre was built in place of their former bed chamber. It became home to a new Royal Dance Company named Silver Steps, and each year the company performed a repertoire of dance from all reaches of the kingdom. A favourite was the Dance of the Invisible Cloak, in which Star had a solo, and Enrico often made a surprise appearance!

A favourite was the Dance of the Invisible Cloak,
in which Star had a solo.

The Princess and the Pea

Long ago, in a land far away, lived Prince Omar. He enjoyed long walks along the river, crevasse jumping, volunteering at the castle library, illuminating manuscripts and making soup. He could do without fire breathing pets, jousting (it was too showy) and spicy food. At least that's what he included in his dating profile.

Dating was much like a play date – you went on outings with lots of new people to learn about them and to try new things. Sometimes you made a great new friend, sometimes there was great romance and sometimes there were just awkward periods of silence. The last kind, the awkward kind, were the sort of dates Prince Omar specialised in. They were dreadful.

For example, his uncle set him up with an endearing witch, but she crashed her broom on the way to their date, and Prince Omar ended up having to take her straight to the royal infirmary. Then a cousin paired Prince Omar with a damsel in distress, but she needed everything done for her, from lifting her soup spoon at dinner to carrying her up her tower steps at the end of the evening. It was exhausting. He met an ogress for luncheon but he slipped and fell in her giant teapot. The last straw came on a date with a werewolf who had tried to hide their true self – the trouble was, Prince Omar had planned an evening hike to view the harvest moon! That time it was the Prince's date who took *him* to the infirmary.

Prince Omar was close to giving up and letting his parents choose for him. This had worked for some of his friends whose parents had a good sense of them. But unfortunately Omar's parents had towering expectations for anyone he dated, and old-fashioned ideas. They had it in their heads he should date a delicate princess.

The Prince mulled it over for the umpteenth time one afternoon, feeling very deflated. Even the weather seemed to share his mood. A great storm was brewing nearby and cast everything into gloom and mist.

Little did Prince Omar know that, just on the other side of the mist, lived an intrepid young princess named Sevinah who shared his struggle.

Princess Sevinah had also tried her hand at dating. The Princess was looking for someone that shared her adventurous spirit, but could be just as happy at home working on a puzzle. She loved cooking, boating, volunteering with gnomes, refreshing

community plots and bogs. She didn't care for scary stories or magic beans.

Princess Sevinah had been on just as many bad dates as Prince Omar. There was The Muffin Man who made fancy cakes, but Princess Sevinah didn't like sweets. She went out with a dragon slayer, but found them too much of a thrill seeker. She thought she may have found a good match in a sorcerer's apprentice, until he tried to impress her at the theatre with a stage-fright spell that went awry, and landed the whole audience in their underwear!

Princess Sevinah, like Prince Omar, desired a break from the pressures of dating, so the same afternoon that the Prince was humming and sighing over his future, she turned her attention to one of her more solitary hobbies – foraging.

Princess Sevinah knew that just beyond the woods near her home was a great river with rushing rapids, and along the river on a wet night glorious mushrooms could be found. Just as the storm commenced, Sevinah carried her boat through the forest to the water like an umbrella. She navigated the rapids like a pro (wearing a helmet of course), getting gloriously soaked. She spotted her favourite fungi along the river bank and drove her vessel ashore.

The princess set right to work, filling her pockets with delicate mushrooms, while she balanced in the boat. She spotted a special morsel just out of reach and while stretching for it, fell face first into the mud. Of course, the boat slipped out from beneath her and drifted away.

Princess Sevinah knew immediately she was stranded, so up she hopped in search of a place to stay, or at least to get some help. As luck would have it, she observed a garden wall in the distance.

Upon reaching the garden, the storm had cleared and the bright moon revealed a glorious palace. Like an invitation, the light was on. (This was actually because Prince Omar had gone to bed with the light on. He was a bit afraid of storms.)

Princess Sevinah rang the bell and was received by the residents of the castle: the King, Queen and a very sleepy Prince Omar.

"Well, what do we have here?" asked the Queen, sticking her nose up at the Princess.

"Good evening, I'm Princess Sevinah," she introduced herself. "I'm sorry to bother you but I lost my boat in the river. I could use a place to clean up and figure out how to get home."

The King and Queen looked her over sceptically. Omar smiled and reached out to shake her hand.

"Are you seriously a princess?" scoffed the King. "You look an awful mess. I've certainly never seen a princess in such disarray."

"Oh, don't be silly. She's clearly a great princess. Come on in and we'll set you up for the night," Prince Omar offered, trying to make up for his parents' bad manners.

"You can stay here, but certainly not in our guest princess suite," said the Queen, looking at the mud dripping on the floor. "We can offer you accommodations in the unrestored tower, I suppose—"

"Mum, that's awful," Prince Omar cut in. "Come this way while my parents get a nicer room ready." He showed Sevinah towards a lounge, shooting the King and Queen serious side-eye on his way out.

"I was just setting up a puzzle as I was having trouble going to sleep during the storm," he said, handing her a towel. "Do you like puzzles, Princess?"

"Why actually I do enjoy a good puzzle," Sevinah confessed. "Thank you."

"What were you doing out there anyway?" asked Omar as they tackled the puzzle. "I love the river… but on a stormy night?"

"Oh, I forage for mushrooms. These conditions are perfect. Plus, I'm sort of taking a break from socialising. Well, dating specifically. I've sort of hit a rut in that area," Sevinah explained.

"Oh, I know just what you mean," Omar nodded. "I've had a stretch of bad luck with it myself."

Over the course of the puzzle (which turned out to be a picture of griffons playing cards), and the course of the evening, the Prince and the Princess talked about their dating woes. The two shared funny stories, embarrassing moments and how hard it was to meet people.

Meanwhile the King and Queen, suspiciously snooping nearby, had taken note of the growing rapport between their son and their muddy guest.

"It looks like—" started the Queen, sourly.

"A date. I know," finished the King. They both sighed. This was not the kind of princess they had in mind for their son. She wasn't delicate or demure. She wasn't passive or overly sensitive. This just wouldn't do.

"We must intervene," stated the King.

"Okay," said the Queen, "but it can't reflect badly on us. . . I know! Omar hates people who are demanding. We must make it seem as if she's impossible to please!"

"Yes, we'll put her through her paces with the worst of sleeping arrangements. Let's put something gross in her mattresses, like, like. . ."

"PEAS!" the Queen squealed. "Yes, then her true colours will show. If she's any kind of princess at all, she'll toss and turn and complain. When she makes such a fuss, Omar's sure to go off her."

"Yes, he hates fuss!" crowed the King.

The King and Queen had got carried away and regretfully hadn't noticed that Prince Omar and Princess Sevinah had not only finished their puzzle, but were just on the other side of the door, listening.

"Come this way," Prince Omar whispered, leading the Princess into a secret passage. "I'm sorry that you had to hear that."

"Not to worry," Princess Sevinah said, "I've been surrounded by those pressures my whole life. But, I think we can beat them at their own game," she proposed, with a gleam in her eye.

"Let's do it!" said Prince Omar, grinning. "You have to pretend to go to sleep, then meet me in this secret passage and hand over the can of peas. I'll take it to their room and tuck it under their bed. Then we'll see what they're made of."

"Time for bed!" announced the King and Queen. Everyone said a royal good night and headed off to their separate chambers. Upon arriving in her room, Princess Sevinah discovered a towering bed laden with dozens of mattresses. Ugh, how was she to know which one was hiding the can of peas?!

After blowing out the candle, Sevinah felt along the wall to locate the door for the secret passage. She found it behind a great tapestry and poked her head though the door.

"Pssst," she signalled to Prince Omar.

"Did you find it already?" whispered the Prince in the distance.

"No. Get in here, it's way more complicated. There's a mountain of mattresses."

Omar sighed and slid along the secret passage wall until he reached Princess Sevinah. Together they silently unpacked each mattress, one by one. Finally, surrounded by down, linen and pillows there – at the very bottom of all the mattresses – was the saddest can of peas.

"Get in here, it's way more complicated."

Princess Sevinah collected the bedding into a cosy nest and enjoyed a great night of sleep. Prince Omar hastened to his parents' room and crept in straight away. He slid his hand beneath the mattress of their great gilded bed and left the offending can. He may have also tucked in a few other things, like a lance, two books, a pair of roller skates and an old loaf of bread. Then Prince Omar slipped back into his room and he too had a great night's rest.

Hours later, the bell rang for breakfast. Princess Sevinah and Prince Omar arrived at the table refreshed and bright, ready to take on the day. The King and Queen, on the other hand, barely appeared at all. The King slunk in wearing a neck brace and his robe on backwards. The Queen arrived with her eye mask over her ears and slippers on her hands, then promptly fell asleep in her breakfast cereal.

"Boy, I slept great, thank you so much," said Princess Sevinah. "But you two don't look very well. Was everything all right last night?"

"I had the worst night's sleep," complained the King. "The mattress was so lumpy it's as if it was made of soggy dough."

The Queen snorted awake. "I wholly disagree! It was so firm it was like sleeping on a stone slab covered in tree roots."

"You know, there must be something funny going on in this castle," said Prince Omar, staring hard at his parents. "Princess Sevinah told me she found a can of peas in her bed, too."

The room fell silent. Only the clatter of silverware could be heard.

From that day forward Princess Sevinah was always welcome at Prince Omar's palace. The King and Queen, having learned the lesson that there is no 'right' kind of princess, and that no single test can determine compatibility, retired to the un-restored tower of the castle to examine their old-fashioned views.

And as for Princess Sevinah and Prince Omar, they remained fast friends and lifelong puzzle buddies. Their conversation that fateful night inspired a joint venture they called Two Peas in a Pod Dating Service, where they delighted in helping people in Fairyland find love and companionship without injury or insult. They even went on some dates with each other – always near the river, always with homemade soup and never an awkward moment of silence.

Zade and the 1001 Ideas

Not all princesses are born into royal leadership. Some climb up and claim it for themselves. This is a story of one such princess, Zade (Zady).

In an ancient land, now buried in dunes and history, there sat a great empire made up of many kingdoms that stretched from sea to sea and mountain to mountain. In this empire lived a great mix of people and magical creatures.

The empire was ruled by a powerful business-minded Sultan who ran it as a company called SESAME Enterprises. The Sultan was an innovator, and through SESAME had created an empire on the cutting edge of technology. He hadn't done it alone, either. For years, he had a business partner. A woman with whom he'd worked alongside, carefully growing SESAME, cultivating a world-renowned reputation.

Then one day, the Sultan's business partner left abruptly for a rival empire on the other side of the world. The Sultan was heartbroken at what he felt was a betrayal. Soon, the company and empire suffered. SESAME's inventions began to fail and the mood in the office was low.

For years many had sought the role of partner, hoping to help run SESAME alongside the Sultan. But the candidates rarely lasted a day, with the moody Sultan finding fault with them and firing them on the spot. Every day the Sultan got up, brushed his teeth, looked in the mirror and complimented himself, then interviewed a candidate for the vacant job of partner, sometimes hiring them – only to come up with a reason they weren't good enough and firing them that same day.

There was Samira, a promising architect, but the Sultan thought her sunglasses were too dark. There was Rajani, who tamed tigers to pull a water wheel, but the Sultan was allergic to cats. There was Kiran, a gifted landscape designer who had plans for an irrigation system, but the Sultan didn't like that she was taller than him.

But Zade was different. She was the daughter of the Sultan's advisor, the vizier. Growing up at the heels of her mother at work, Zade had access to the company archives. In fact, that was where she spent most of her free time. Zade perused all the books, and collected in her memory many tales of history, poetry, philosophy, sciences and the arts. This made Zade wise, witty, inventive, well read and a great candidate for a job at SESAME.

Zade's mother was against the idea. She worked closely with the Sultan and knew well his petty, whiny ways. But Zade was confident. Plus, she had an idea. So, finally her mother agreed to secure her an interview in the Sultan's office chambers.

Zade arrived at the great palace. Inside, the halls were eerily silent. Zade passed empty desks, dusty plants and blank chalkboards on her way to the interview. It was like a cemetery, no wonder the company was lacking inspiration and creativity.

Zade found the Sultan pouting behind his desk. She cleared her throat.

"Show me what you've got so I can dismiss you already," the Sultan waved airily. "What makes you think you have something my great mind doesn't? Pitch me!"

Zade took a deep breath, "Well… May I start with a story, of a product no one can do without?"

The Sultan was tired after months of failure and firings. "A story? I haven't got time for stories," he said grumpily, making to get up.

Zade blocked his way. "Picture yourself alone in the village. All your worldly possessions in a tiny house. This is how many of our country folk live."

"What does this have to do with SESAME enterprises?" puzzled the Sultan.

But Zade pressed on. "Outside rove bands of thieves on horseback. Throughout the night you can hear the hooves like the rattling of a cage. Imagine yourself, stepping away from home, fearing for your property, friends and neighbours already struck by thieves, their livelihoods lost. How can you ever find peace of mind?"

The Sultan listened as Zade pitched her invention through an elaborate tale of 40 thieves that strike villages in the dead of night, citizens trembling in fear, nothing to stop them. The day passed into afternoon and then evening, until Zade noticed the time and stopped in the middle of her pitch.

"Tomorrow I'll share with you the blueprint I've created for a state-of-the-art security system to beat thieves. It links villages with law enforcement, and dispatches dragons!"

"I want to see the plans now," said the Sultan.

"Oh no, look at the time. I'd be happy to finish the pitch tomorrow. I'll be here bright and early." With that Zade walked out of the office.

Her mother had been waiting for her outside and peppered her with questions. "What happened? You were in there for ages. Did you get hired? Did you get fired?"

"The Sultan will have me back tomorrow," Zade said with a wink.

And he did. The following morning, Zade showed up bright and early at the palace just as she planned and strode into the board room. There she found the Sultan an eager audience. She finished the pitch with a big reveal, a working demo. First Zade sprinkled fine sand around a mysterious box. Then a hired pickpocket appeared and swiped a necklace of jewels. All of a sudden, light erupted from the box, the sand formed into a mound and became a dragon, who seized the pickpocket immediately.

The Sultan was impressed, but he didn't show it. He simply raised his eyebrows and asked, "Is that all you've got?"

"Oh, of course not, that is just the start." Zade pressed on. "I've another invention developing that I think is right up your alley. Have you ever had a clumsy friend or family member?" Zade spun off a story all about epic klutzes, lost left shoes, keys left in locks and all sorts of foolishness.

"This is called FoolProof and will keep a person from getting in their own way. We lose much time and money to inefficiency. This will revolutionise the everyday. No more searching for a to-do list or emptying your pockets looking for—"

"What's with all this talk? It's getting late, when can I see the prototype?" interrupted the Sultan.

"Oh, it is late indeed," piped Zade in fake surprise. "Well we will just have to finish this tomorrow." And she packed up her things and zipped out of the room before the Sultan could object.

Zade arrived the following day and finished the pitch with a fancy prototype for a gadget that one wore on the wrist, which emitted a tiny trail to a number of personal belongings. Whenever the wearer needed anything they would simply tap a glistening thread and the desired item would appear.

Before the Sultan could catch his breath, she launched right into another invention. She'd already captured the Sultan's attention far longer than anyone else and she wasn't going to give him a moment to even think about firing her. She knew she was qualified, challenged and eager for the position of partner. Zade also knew SESAME Enterprises hung in the balance and she had a chance to save it.

The next idea she described was a love potion that came in a special lamp. When a person rubbed the surface it collected their true heart's desire and emitted a pink mist whenever that person neared a good match. That proposal turned into the next, which turned into the next, and before long hundreds of inventions had been proposed.

With each hour, the Sultan kept Zade on. First as a candidate, then as an intern, and as her inventions and ideas were put into being, he was forced to make her an associate. The Sultan eagerly anticipated the finishing of the previous day's idea, invention, pitch or story. Zade had carefully researched safety kits that deployed a genie to help those in distress; tents that could also be coats; an aqueduct that served a great desert; even a chariot pulled by trained birds to help conserve energy. And in these inventions the Sultan found a match for his creativity.

As Zade reached the top of SESAME industries she had one last hurdle to jump to get to the top. The job she had sought all along. Partner.

For this final story, which happened to be number 1001, Zade brought out her bravest moves yet. She reserved a larger conference room and when the Sultan sat down, she announced, "We will do this in just one sitting."

"We?" the Sultan wondered aloud.

Zade then opened the door of the conference room and invited in two other staff members. "For this presentation, I'll need some assistance. You see, the most ambitious ideas take many minds and here at SESAME I happened upon some of the greatest. Once there was a young Prince poised to be the Sultan," Zade started bravely. The Sultan furrowed his brow. "He had two sisters. The three siblings fought all the time to impress their parents, always stepping on each other's shoulders to get the most attention. Their parents were tired of their nonsense and sent them on an epic quest to teach them a lesson." Zade and her colleagues laid out three key items; an apple, a telescope and a rolled-up rug. "This is Liya. She'll present the first idea."

Liya stepped forward, "The first sister's journey took her to a monastery where she was awarded an apple of wisdom during a test of conscience! We could really make this." She held up the apple and it opened in sections, revealing maps and letters and computations. "It would be like a library in the palm of your hand."

Zade's eyes lit up. The Sultan's did as well.

"And next we have Rose." Zade introduced her other colleague.

Rose raised the telescope. "The other sister met a monstrous troll on her journey, who she wrestled and won an all-seeing telescope – an expert navigation device that could show the user to their loved ones anywhere in the world."

"Rose's engineering team could start on this right now," Zade proclaimed. "The last sibling, the young Prince, had spurned offers of help along his journey and found himself lost in an unfriendly marketplace. He cried out for help and his sisters heard him. One used the apple of wisdom to discover his location, and the other used the telescope to navigate the way to him. He was so relieved to be reunited with his sisters, they agreed to stop their quarrelling and be stronger together. Just as they embraced, the carpet they were standing upon lifted magically in the air and swept the trio home to their family." Zade unfurled the rug in a grand gesture. "We could make this magic carpet with our team of textile conjurers here at SESAME."

The Sultan nearly applauded. "These are the most inspired, cutting-edge ideas," he said, stepping towards Zade. He put his hands together to clap, then extended one to her to shake. "I wasted too much time being threatened by those who wanted to work beside me. Your work, and the work of everyone here has rebuilt this company. If you'll accept the position as partner in SESAME Enterprises, I'd be so grateful."

"I'd be delighted," Zade shook the Sultan's hand, "on one condition. It's time to rebrand. I'd like to call the company 'OPEN SESAME: minds open for business'."

And with that, the empire had a new leadership team. Together Zade and the Sultan revolutionised the lives of those around them and helped nurture young inventors, no matter how dark their glasses were, how tall or strong – so long as they had great ideas and believed in a little bit of magic.

"*These are the most inspired, cutting-edge ideas,*"
said the Sultan.

Thumbelina

There once was a woman who lived on a faraway island amongst jungles, lagoons, volcanoes and a great seashore. The woman wished very much to have a child. So, she visited Barley, Corn and Associates, a prominent magical and medicinal clinic, and was given the opportunity to raise a flower child.

These small children were grown inside flowers and the woman was sent home with a seedling. She potted her flower and kept it healthy and nourished. One day, when she leaned in to kiss the blossom, it opened to reveal a tiny girl inside.

The woman was overjoyed and named her new daughter Mai. She set up a clever home for her tiny daughter with a sea-shell bed, a thimble chair and table and a boat made from banana leaves and the whiskers of a tiger. Every night, the woman would sing to Mai and the two would make up rhymes together. Mai grew to be a great lover of music. She invented stringed instruments from stems and grasses and percussion from seed pods and sand. She carved holes in twigs to make flutes and brushed dew drops along the rim of polished sea glass. Mai imagined it sounded like the wings of tiny fairies.

Mai's music soon attracted attention. Animals and people alike would stop outside her home to hear her play.

One day, Mai's mother interrupted her playing with a suggestion. "How'd you like a wider audience for your music? There's only so much our small town can offer. A bigger place could give you the chance to be a star."

Mai considered the idea. True, her town was lovely, but she was always curious what else was out there, and a chance to develop her music in an exciting new town sounded promising. Mai was sad to leave but she packed her instruments in her sea-shell bed and set off in the direction of the next biggest town. Before she left, her mother hugged her tight and said, "Remember, Mai, always ask questions. You don't have to trust someone until they've earned it."

After travelling for some time, Mai stopped by a pond to make camp. Just as she was closing her eyes, she heard a voice behind her.

"Well, aren't you a sight, missy," hissed a creaky voice.

"Who's there?" asked Mai.

"Well hello, Dearie." A large toad slunk out

from the shadows. "I do believe you are on my property." She brandished a stick thick with neon algae that dripped over Mai as the toad moved closer.

"Oh, I'm sorry, I'll pack up straight away," Mai said, jumping out of the shell.

The slimy creature reached into the shell and caressed a flute. "No need my pet, you can be Lady Toad's guest," and she trod off with Mai's belongings in hand. Mai had no choice but to follow.

In Lady Toad's residence it was clear something was not right. She fussed and fawned over Mai, touching her hair, poking her ribs.

"Just what are you doing out alone on a night like this?" coaxed Lady Toad.

"I'm off to pursue my dream of being a musician," Mai said proudly.

"It's as if you fell right into my lap!" Lady Toad said triumphantly. "Our family has a travelling band. How'd you like a spot in our show? I'll make you a flashy costume and you can perform in the late show every night. Only the finest critters come out at that hour. We'll be rich!"

Mai doubted that the finest folks came out in the wee hours. She desperately wanted to leave, but Lady Toad had her shell and all her instruments. Mai was sick to her stomach. What had she stumbled into?

"Allow me to show you to your, um, quarters," offered Lady Toad, gesturing to a far-off lily pad. Lady Toad hopped her way over to the middle of the pond and dumped Mai onto the slippery pad. She brushed all nearby leaves or stepping stones aside and disappeared into the dark, leaving Mai stranded.

Mai was frightened. She couldn't swim and was too small to reach anything nearby to escape. Trying to comfort herself, she put her hands in her pockets and discovered a bit of sea glass. Mai dipped a finger into the murky pond water, then slid it along the glass and began to play a mournful song.

Below her a fish, stirred by Mai's music, popped its head out of the water.

"What a sad tune," the fish noted. "Is something the matter?"

Mai explained her predicament. "I'm supposed to be headed to a big city to be a musician, but Lady Toad put me here," she said, gesturing to the lily pad. "I'm stuck with nowhere to go."

"I'm very sorry to hear of your troubles. I can't do much, but I can cut you loose," said the fish. It nibbled the stem of the lily pad until it cut loose and Mai began to float.

"My friends the butterflies will help you. Just look up!" called the fish. "They'll guide you to dry land."

"Thank you," Mai called back, grabbing a stick as a paddle.

Mai propelled the boat along the water as it opened

to a stream. When the night sky gave way to dawn she saw a tangle of lovely butterflies on the horizon. She followed them just as the fish had suggested, and the stream turned to a marsh and then a field. Mai stepped off the lily pad onto dry land.

Parrot calls filled the sky above and they kept Mai awake as she strode through the field. She was very tired but she flicked the grasses in rhythm with the bird's voice and wrote a new song to keep her company as she journeyed.

Soon, Mai arrived at a small door in the field. She was exhausted and without a single belonging, so she gave the door a rapid pound, eager to rouse the owner.

An old dotty mouse answered the door.

"Come in from the cold, young thing," the mouse invited.

The mouse was welcoming and tended to Mai, keeping her warm and fed. Mai offered to return the favour by singing.

"You're a musician?" inquired the mouse.

"Well, I'm working at it. I was on my way to the next biggest town to see if I have what it takes," Mai explained.

Mai sang a song that she'd written for the mouse, accompanying herself on the sea glass. It was marvellous and the mouse applauded generously.

"I know just who to introduce you to," declared the mouse. "My neighbour, Lord Mole. He knows all the top talent in music." And with that, the mouse ran next door to Lord Mole's. She was gone for quite some time, and when she returned she looked very proud of herself.

"It's all set, pet. Lord Mole is anxious to meet you."

Mai barely had a moment to protest, for the mouse took Mai by the hand and led her down her tunnel to her neighbour. "He'll keep you in fancy clothes, pay for your music career and introduce you to all sorts of important critters. I've already signed a contract for you," the mouse prattled.

Along the way they passed a bird, collapsed in a heap.

"Don't mind the riff raff," the mouse gestured to the feathered mass. "Once you're a famous singer, all your paths will be cleared."

"Welcome," beckoned Lord Mole when they arrived at his underground office. The walls were littered with awards, album covers and photos featuring the smiling faces of his friends and clients. Everything looked a little too good to be true.

"Step over here, let me take a look at you," Lord Mole coaxed, circling Mai. He talked endlessly about lords and ladies, barons and baronesses, and all manner of fancy folk. Mai remembered what her mother said. She didn't trust Lord Mole one bit.

"We'll start with a makeover. I'll order you a new wardrobe made exclusively of dragonfly wings, to show off your cute little self." Lord Mole began dictating a

Mai remembered what her mother had said.
She didn't trust Lord Mole one bit.

list to the mouse. "With shoes to make you taller, of course. We'll give you a tragic backstory, too. What was it you said, you were born in a burned-out hazelnut shell…?"

"Uh no, I'm from a beautiful flower," Mai tried to interrupt.

"I'll have Spotted Newt write you some new tracks. He's tapped into all the trends," Lord Mole continued.

"But I write my own music," Mai said.

Lord Mole laughed loudly. "Success in this business is not about your lyrics, it's about the whole package. And I know just how to wrap you up. Trust me!"

Mai was beginning to see the full extent of Lord Mole's plan and none of it included her music. He'd never even heard her sing! Mai was fed up, so she faked a yawn and excused herself back to the mouse house. She had to figure a way out of this.

On the way, Mai stopped beside the overcome bird, a beautiful parrot.

"Are you alright?" she asked as she knelt beside the poor creature.

"I could use a hand, I caught something in my wing on my way out of town," the parrot explained.

"Ah, I think I heard you before, singing. I was so inspired," said Mai.

"Oh, so was that you on the accompaniment?" smiled the parrot.

Mai smiled back, then examined the wounded bird. "There's a thorn in your wing," she explained. "There's been a thorn in my side as well."

"I'd be glad to help you with yours if you help me with mine. But I don't see anything on ya," said the parrot.

"It's not a real one," Mai laughed, rolling the parrot on his side, then gently loosening the offending thorn. "You see, I set off to find the next great place to pursue my music. But everyone I've met so far wants to change me in a way that suits them. The latest is a mouse who signed me into a contract with Lord Mole, but something about him doesn't sit right with me. That's my thorn."

"Sounds like you have good instincts. That contract sounds fishy, especially since you didn't even sign it. I think I know a way to get you out of it all. You've helped me with my thorn, now it's my turn to help you," said the parrot.

On the morning of Mai's makeover, all the critters Lord Mole had hired arrived with him at the mouse's house. Just as Lord Mole was about to leave, Mai said, "Lord Mole, you've hired this big team for me, don't you want to hear me sing?" Lord Mole paused at the door. "To show everyone how great I'm going to be, how rich I'll make them all?"

"Oh, of course." Lord Mole glowed at the sound of riches.

So, Mai reached for a set of pots to use as drums, plucked a comb from the table to play across her lips and set about playing and singing the single most. . . *awful* song anyone had ever heard.

"LAAAAAAAA, la la la la la la la leeeeeeee!" Mai screeched, hamming it up.

The creatures in the burrow covered their ears, some covered their eyes and those that didn't exchanged wide-eyed looks. When the song was over, Mai dropped the comb, clattered the pots to the floor and strode out of the burrow, head held high. Lord Mole took after Mai. "You'll never be a star with shenanigans like that!"

"Watch me!" said Mai.

Lord Mole shook his fist at her in anger, but at just that moment the freshly healed parrot swooped from the sky and picked Mai up, up and away.

Together they flew a day's journey and the parrot landed in a kingdom of flowers at the doorstep of a place called the Wings of Music Residency Centre.

"Ta da!" announced the parrot. "This is what your heart desires, am I right?"

"Oh my, it's wonderful," Mai said.

The institute was like a grand park, with small cottages for studios, instrument making and performing. Fairies, critters and creatures of all kinds mingled through the grounds, whistling, singing and tapping out rhythms. Even some just Mai's size!

"It's a place where you'll always be the author of your own song," explained the parrot.

"No one to push me into contracts, performances or costumes!" cheered Mai. She gave the parrot a tremendous hug and sent him on his way. "Thank you, thank you!" Mai waved as he flew off.

Mai remained at the residency for a long time, exploring her craft, inventing instruments and making lifelong friends. Many of her friends had similar stories about having been mistreated and misdirected in their pursuits as artists.

When Mai left the residency, she became a prominent musical producer, helping magical creatures foster their gifts and preserve the integrity of their work. In later life, she retrained as a lawyer specialising in contracts and advocacy. She fought tirelessly for even the smallest creature, ensuring they too could follow their heart.

Little Red Riding Hood

Once upon a time, deep in the heart of the country, there lived three generations of women: Granny Fran, Mama Felice and her daughter Filipa. For years, the family lived in a cosy village beside a great wood. The villagers coexisted peacefully with the animals in the woods – rabbits and deer, foxes and squirrels, a variety of birds and a pack of stunning grey wolves. As the top predators, the wolves helped keep all the other animals healthy and strong and the forest vibrant and green.

Throughout the years the village grew bigger and bigger, eating into the woods. The balance between people and animals shifted. As the wolves had fewer places to live and fewer things to eat, they started to steal food and farm animals from humans.

One day, when Mama Felice was a child, she came face-to-face with a pair of wolves while on an errand. They barred her path and twitched their pointy ears.

"My, what big ears you have," she whispered.

The wolves stepped towards her.

"My, what big eyes you have," she said as she leaned back.

The wolves bared their teeth and sniffed the air.

"My, what big teeth you have," she gasped.

Luckily for her, a hunting party was nearby. They caught a glimpse of her red headband and scooped her up to safety.

From that day forth the family told this tale and cautioned other families in the village against sending children into the woods alone. Granny Fran fashioned a bright-red hooded cape for her daughter Felice to wear on outings so adults in the area could watch out for her.

When Felice had her daughter Filipa she was quick to remind her of the wolves. She cautioned her to avoid the woods, and to always wear her bright red cape when she was out walking. This is how she got the name, Little Red. As years passed, the village grew larger still, and the forest grew smaller and more dangerous. Instead of travelling through the feared woods, the villagers built the new homes around it. Granny Fran, sad to see the woods disappear and the village overtaking them, moved one winter to a more remote cottage.

While Granny Fran was busy unpacking in her new home, Mama Felice asked her daughter, "Filipa dear, can you please bring Granny a few items?"

"Of course, Mum," Filipa said, always glad to help. "I'll just finish feeding the birds." Filipa often cared for the wildlife, especially in the colder months.

"I've put together a basket with a crusty baguette, a bottle of milk, a stick of butter and a log of cured meats," Mama Felice explained, hanging the basket on Filipa's arm. "If you leave soon you can get there before dark, as it's a long way round the woods."

"But if I cut through the trees it's a quicker trip," suggested Filipa.

Mama Felice regarded her daughter sternly. "We never use the path through the woods. You remember what happened to me, right?"

"I know, I know, Mother. The wolves," Filipa obliged. "Never get close enough to see what pointy ears they have, what big eyes they have and what sharp teeth they have," she recited.

"And the best way to avoid wolves, is to go around and stay on the path," Mama Felice added. "Oh, and don't forget the red cape!" she called after Filipa as she stepped to the door.

Filipa grabbed the heirloom red cape from the coat stand, slung it round her shoulders and stepped out onto the wintry trail. She looked like a holly berry in the snow. As Filipa walked along, a stiff wind blew the snowflakes in a swirling white screen, making it difficult to see. As she neared the place where the road forked, one way leading round the woods and the other leading straight through it, Filipa could scarcely work out which way to go. She sniffed the air and groped in the blinding snow. "I think this is the way," she remarked, as she chose the trail that went through the woods.

As she walked, pine needles crunched beneath her feet, animals scurried about and the wind died down, revealing to Filipa that she was in the woods.

"Oh shoot. Well at least this will be quicker," she said to herself. But just then a strange feeling befell Filipa.

She lowered the hood on her cape so she could listen more closely to her surroundings and what she heard gave her pause. Something else was breathing heavily nearby. She heard weighty foot

falls and eerily, she heard small animals scurry away from where she stood.

She narrowed her eyes and peered into the woods around her, starting on her left. As Filipa turned her head to the right, she saw a pair of pointy ears in the trees. Filipa's breath caught in her chest. She stepped towards the ears, and two glowing eyes revealed themselves between the bare tree branches.

She knew from her care of other woodland animals not to stare the animal down, and not to run. Instead, very slowly, Filipa reached into her grocery basket and withdrew the bottle of milk. Holding it like a spear she thrust it at what she now knew to be a wolf!

A second wolf emerged beside it and so again to her basket Filipa went, this time for the cold stick of butter. She threw it at the feet of the snarling wolves who regarded it curiously. Filipa then took the baguette, raised it above her head like a sword, and took the opportunity to slowly inch back from the wolves. She walked backwards, all the way to the fork in the trail, holding her breath.

Once she was safely out of the wolves' range, Filipa remembered her Granny! Quick as she could she secured her hood, ditched the basket and ran with the cured meats in one hand and the baguette in the other all the way around the woods to Granny Fran's new house.

She arrived panting and sweaty just as the moon was rising. And to her surprise the door to Granny's new cottage was ajar.

"Granny, are you in?" Filipa knocked lightly on the door and it swung open.

Inside she was greeted with an unfathomable sight. Two wolves, their faces dappled with milk and their paws greasy with butter, slipped and slid on the floor. Filipa's grandmother was perched atop an armoire, brandishing a fireplace iron.

Filipa brought the baguette and cured meats up above her head like two swords. The wolves sniffed the air and turned, noses first, to confront her.

"Lure them outside!" shouted Granny Fran.

"What?" wavered Filipa.

"The food, my dear!" Her grandmother nodded to the baguette and cured meat.

Filipa looked from the wolves to her hands where she held tightly to her food swords. A flash of recognition crossed her face and she flung the food behind her into the garden. The wolves darted on either side of Filipa to reach the food and as they did they kicked the air up around her, sending her cape spinning. In the garden, the wolves pounced like puppies on the bread and the meat. Devouring the food eagerly, they paid no attention to Filipa or her grandmother.

"The door, dear," Granny Fran interrupted Filipa's observation of the wolves. Filipa quickly bolted the door and helped her grandmother down from the armoire.

"Shall I call for some help, Granny?"

"I'd say the ones who need help are those wolves. They are very hungry. And they really shouldn't have a taste for human food."

"You're right, they are hungry," Filipa murmured, watching the animals again from the window. "What about all the rabbits and deer they usually eat? Have they eaten them all?"

"No, no my child," said Granny Fran. "There haven't been enough deer or rabbits for a long time. Not since the village took over all the land. Those other animals have few places to live and so the wolves have less to eat."

"How awful," reflected Filipa, sitting next to her grandmother. "What can we do to bring back the rabbits and deer?"

"Why don't you write to the Fairyland Environmental Bureau (FEB)? They'll appreciate a plucky young voice like yours and help us keep the wolves and the village safe."

So as Granny Fran built a fire, Filipa drafted a letter. She outlined her family's history with the wolves, her own encounter and the turn of events at her grandmother's house. She fetched Granny Fran's quickest carrier pigeon, Lars, and

sent her request into the air.

The two eagerly awaited a response. And the next day they got it, in the form of a visit from the FEB Wolf Response Team. Together Granny Fran and Filipa helped the team examine animal tracks, collect crumbs and look for signs of the wolves. All the wolves in the forest would be tracked and relocated, the team explained, because they were no longer safe around humans.

"It's sad that there won't be wolves in our forest any more. How can we make this area better so they can come back?" Filipa asked, as the team packed up.

"What an excellent question," the team leader said. "You can help grow the forest by planting trees. That will bring the animals and plants back to the area and then we can bring the wolves back safely. We have a Junior Ranger Programme, if you're really serious?"

Filipa grinned. "I'd really like that. I'd hate to have to move because there wasn't enough to eat. The animals shouldn't have to move, either."

The FEB Wolf Response Team departed but not before giving Filipa a series of books and maps, a special tracker's guide and a beacon for exploring the woods safely.

"If you study hard you'll be a junior ranger in no time!" the team called back, as they loped silently on snowshoes into the woods.

In the months that followed, Filipa stayed with her Granny Fran and diligently studied her junior ranger materials. She tracked prints, followed her nose, memorised the multitude of ecosystems that coexisted in her area and educated others in the village about the cause of the wolves.

She finished the studies in record time and was sworn in that summer as the youngest junior forest ranger in the FEB. Filipa volunteered each weekend with the FEB and of course had her sights set on the Wolf Response Team.

Just a few years later she led that very team, and was once again reunited with the wolves. She worked to relocate wolves who grew too close to humans, and even cared for a cub that had been injured. From that day forward Filipa dedicated her life to forestry conservation, with special consideration for wolves.

Later, while raising a daughter of her own, Filipa campaigned for the rights of wolves in the wild. And after the wolves returned to her home region, she successfully appealed to make the hunting of wolves in Fairyland illegal. Years later, when she herself was called Granny Filipa, she was honoured by the Fairyland Environmental Bureau with the title of Faithful Friend of the Forest. However, most people just referred to her as Princess of the Wolves.

She even cared for a cub that had been injured.

Sleeping Beauty

Once a long, long time ago there were two kingdoms that sat, like twins, side by side in a great and beautiful landscape. Just like real twins, sometimes they got along, and sometimes they bickered, yet they always looked out for one another.

One kingdom had just had an heir – a nice little kiddo named Filipp. The kings that ruled the other kingdom were eager to share their love with a baby of their own, too, and with the help of their court clerk, adopted a lovely baby girl. They couldn't wait to welcome her into their family, and woke before the sun on the day of her arrival. It is for this reason that they named her Aurora, meaning 'dawn'.

They had a big party for darling Aurora and invited everyone they could think of, including the fairies and magical creatures that looked out for everyone's well-being.

However, there was one person they had forgotten. Most people wouldn't show up to a party if they hadn't been invited, but this person did. She arrived just as the fairies were giving gifts by casting dazzling spells on the young Princess. She herself was a fairy, coarse and grouchy, and so sensitive to the sun she could only come out on cloudy days. Her dark-brimmed hat and glasses gave an unfriendly 'don't talk to me' impression, and everyone called her the Cloud Fairy. The Cloud Fairy pushed her way to the head of the line and scolded the kings for being left off the guest list.

The kings looked to each other pleadingly. Which one of them had messed up? It was an unintentional oversight, they tried to explain. The Cloud Fairy should certainly feel welcome, they offered. "Ha! Where could I even sit amongst all this sunlight?!" shouted the party crasher.

The kings tried to apologise, but the damage was done. The Cloud Fairy crept close to the Princess's bassinet. "Just as I have been cursed with a difference that makes my

life difficult, so shall the Princess!" she proclaimed, casting her spell. "So your family will know how hard it is to go about the world in loneliness and isolation; without friends or party invites; without beach days and sunny parades, I curse the Princess with a condition of inconvenient and overwhelming sleep! Sleep that shall befall her at all hours and keep her from enjoying life's parties! And if the Princess should try and fight it, she will run the risk of pricking her finger, as a teenager, on something sharp, and falling asleep forever!"

With that, the Cloud Fairy stormed out in a huff. Everyone let out the breath they had been holding.

"Well, that was awkward," noted the trio of fairies who had been at the Princess's side just before the party crasher arrived. "We'll see what we can do about that curse." But try as they might, the three fairies could not undo the spell, and right there in the midst of the festivities, Aurora dozed off. Looking at each other worriedly, they turned to the kings.

"We can't cure Aurora," they said, "but we can look after her. We know a great sleep clinic in the woods. If you like, we can move Aurora there, and make sure she gets the best help possible."

The kings weighed the matter. While they would be so sad to be without Aurora, as parents they wanted the best for her, so they agreed. Aurora would go and live at the sleep clinic with the trio of fairies.

As Aurora grew up in the sleep clinic, she tried to enjoy the typical fun a young princess might have. However, she would often grow weary and fall asleep. During her gardening, she would wake up in flower beds and wheel barrows. At swimming outings, she would doze on lily pads and float downstream, once coming inches from a waterfall! The sleeping curse also made it hard to have friends over. During tea parties she would slumber while the tea steeped. During birthdays, she would wilt into the cake. Soon, invitations ceased to arrive. While she always had her steadfast buddy since she was a baby, her neighbour Prince Filipp (who was often the only one left awake at their play dates), and her parents and the fairies, who remained ever so patient, she often felt low.

As Aurora grew, she realised her sleeping troubles weren't going to go away, and began to desire more information about them. Together with Filipp and the trio of fairies, the kings encouraged Aurora in her quest to learn about her difference by bringing in books and scrolls, magic mirrors and crystal balls. Aurora was a quick learner and started her own napping routine, which everyone benefitted from. She managed her own diet and nutrition plan, and built a fitness centre in the cottage to stay strong and combat the spell.

Soon, Aurora started publishing her own papers on her experience with a sleep disorder. She even began advanced coursework to become a physician herself, and others in the kingdom were eager to learn from her, inviting her for speaking engagements and conferences.

Unfortunately, this meant the Cloud Fairy too learned of Aurora's confidence and resiliency, and set in motion a plan to interrupt it. For the Cloud Fairy had warned Aurora's family that if she sought to improve her condition, she would fall into a sleep to last a lifetime.

Spurned by her own unhappiness, the Cloud Fairy followed through on her threat, and set a trap for the teenage princess. While out for a walk in the woods to meet Filipp, something caught Aurora's eye. It was an abandoned barn, filled with tools for all sorts of hobbies Aurora hadn't the time or waking hours to enjoy.

There were musical instruments and an art studio, a wood shop and a fibre craft corner; complete with wool to be carded, a loom and a spinning wheel to make thread. Aurora, ever curious, explored eagerly. The place was a bit of a wreck, with many sharp splintery edges, and flecks of flax, wool and bits of wood everywhere. In no time, Aurora tripped over a fallen stool and pricked her finger on the spinning wheel, getting a splinter.

Filipp and the trio of fairies were accustomed to Aurora's rigid schedule and when she did not appear as expected, they raced to find her. They soon arrived outside the hobby barn, where they found Aurora lying in a deep sleep. Nearby, hidden in the shadows, the Cloud Fairy watched on.

Aurora was moved from the scene of the incident, back to her fathers' castle. She was made comfortable in her childhood chambers and all the experts from the sleep clinic and the kingdoms were brought in to work tirelessly on a cure. They published Aurora's very own papers and research, calling for anyone with similar conditions to come forward.

The sharing of Aurora's struggle, in her own words, had a magical effect. For it inspired people and magical creatures all around the kingdom to begin to share their stories of what made them different, and how they had struggled, too. They drew courage from Aurora's example, and began to speak up for what they needed and to teach one another about their differences.

All around the kingdom were conversations of compassion and care, of accommodation and welcome. And these conversations reached even the darkest corners, including the corner where the Cloud Fairy lived. She began to ponder, had her curse backfired? Were the things that made everyone different the very things that brought them together? "Was there a world where everyone could be included after all?" she wondered aloud. Even her?

There was only one way to find out. The Cloud Fairy would have to risk it all. So once again she descended upon the palace of the kings. Upon her arrival, she snuck into the castle and crept, hidden by shadows, up to Aurora's chamber.

Upon seeing Aurora, the Cloud Fairy was overcome. For she saw Aurora just as she had felt all her life: isolated and alone. She knew at once what she needed to do, and that only she had the power to do it.

The Cloud Fairy stepped bravely forward, wincing with the discomfort of the light. Filipp, who was often checking in on his friend, happened upon the two and rushed in. The Cloud Fairy worried that he meant to harm her, but to her surprise Filipp opened a parasol above her head to shield her from the light. The two took up position beside Aurora. "Is there anything you can do?" Filipp inquired.

The Cloud Fairy nodded. "I should have done this a long time ago," she murmured, gently lifting Aurora's injured hand and removing the offending splinter.

Aurora let out a generous yawn and opened her eyes. "I feel as though I've been asleep for ages."

"You have my dear," replied the fairy, "and it was all my doing. I played a nasty trick on you and I am so sorry. I felt so left out and I just wanted someone else to know what that feels like. But you've shown me that we don't have to hide what makes us different. We can help each other – all we have to do is ask."

Aurora offered the fairy a generous and forgiving hug, for she truly understood. "What do they call you?" she asked.

"Oh, I'm Jewel," said the Cloud Fairy. "I haven't felt like one recently but you, Aurora, have brought light back into my life. And I feel once again that I can live up to my name."

Now that Aurora was awake, a great celebration was held at the palace and this time, no one was forgotten. Shortly thereafter, Filipp and Aurora took over leadership of their kingdoms and set to work making them a united place – an example of inclusion. Aurora and Jewel founded The Centre for the Study of Sleep and Circadian Differences, and were pioneers in creating a place where everyone was encouraged to be themselves, and help others to be their best selves.

And in this kingdom, united by compassion, where everyone made space for one another and celebrated differences, they really did live happily ever after.

*Aurora offered the fairy a generous and forgiving hug,
for she truly understood.*

Snow White

Once upon a time there was a family, made of King White, Queen White and his daughter from a prior marriage, Princess Neve White. They lived in a lovely kingdom near woods and streams, dotted with woodworking shops that made all manner of marvels.

One day, the King set off on a worldwide tour to care for soldiers wounded in battle. With the King away, the Queen took over all royal duties and public appearances. This included arts events, hospital openings, speaking engagements, ribbon cuttings, parades, races, charitable work, photoshoots, state dinners – the works. At first it was fun. However, as time went on, the Queen realised people were more interested in what she looked like than what she did. Headlines included: *Best Dressed List: is our Queen on it?* and the rather more unkind: *The Queen's Dress Disaster: what was she thinking? Emerald is a young person's colour.* Eventually, the time the Queen once spent preparing speeches, she instead spent poring over magazines. The time the Queen once spent researching key causes, she instead used to sample lotions and potions with labels such as Ageless Serum, Wrinkle Evaporator, Skin Perfecto and Blemish Blaster. And instead of arriving early to an event, the Queen took extra time to talk to her reflection in the mirror. Mostly she said mean things to herself. So much so, that one day her mirror broke in protest.

The Queen had seen an advertisement for a newfangled truth-telling Magic Mirror. Fairest Fortune it was called. It talked to the user and told it generous compliments.

"Ooooh," murmured the Queen, "this is just what I need with my big Magical Creatures event coming up. I'll really want to land on the Dressed Better Than the Rest list." So she ordered it the very next day.

Down the castle hall from the Queen lived her stepdaughter, Princess Neve White. She didn't have to attend events with her stepmother, so with her free time she read newspapers and stories of brave princes and princesses the world over. The Princess also enjoyed lotions and potions, but hers included face paints and hair chalk, plus daring combinations such as lemon yellow curls and glitter stars. As she was so open and interested in others, a princess from another kingdom shared her custom of henna patterns with Neve. The Queen wasn't impressed by Snow White's experimenting.

"Don't you want to cinch in your waist? There will be pictures taken," the Queen queried when they dressed for an outing.

"But then I can't breathe," Neve replied.

"You should have a little less coal around your eyes. You'll look old," the Queen

said while passing by the Princess at her vanity.

"Don't you mean wise?" Neve questioned.

"That loud lipstick will bring all the wrong attention," said the Queen another time.

"Well, I like it," said Neve.

One day a parcel arrived at the castle. The Queen and the Princess raced to get it.

"It's my Medusa Hair Care Kit!" shouted Princess Neve, racing down the stairs.

"It's for me," said the Queen coolly. "It's my Fairest Fortune Mirror. You wouldn't have any use for it. It's for people who actually put care into their appearance."

"I'm just having fun. Why are you always so harsh?" asked the Princess quietly.

"Fun?!" yelled the Queen. "You think make-up and hair and all the rest is fun? It's survival, my dear. I've had my ears staked back; I've taken foul-tasting elixirs to turn my hair to gold; I've used burning serums to keep my teeth white; I've trained moths to set about my face to give me the most enchanting eyelashes."

"But… why?" Neve asked, shocked at what she'd heard.

"As Queen, I have to look perfect," she choked back tears. "I wouldn't expect you to understand. Just leave me alone, I have to focus on my next event appearance!"

"There's no such thing as perfect," Princess Neve whispered to herself. To cool things off, she packed her bags for a campout in the woodlands.

Once in the woods, Neve came upon a cute dwelling, complete with seating and lodging for seven. Thinking it an inn, Princess Neve set about making herself at home, and even lay down for a nap. When she awoke, Princess Neve discovered it was not an inn but instead a boarding house for gnomes. Seven to be exact! They were a merry bunch and eager to talk to their guest. "What brings you here?" one asked.

"I'm Princess Neve White," said Neve, "and I live with my stepmother the Queen. We've not been getting on lately, so I wanted to give her some space. Can I stay for a night or two?"

The gnomes welcomed the Princess with open arms.

Back at the palace, the Queen tried out her Fairest Fortune Mirror.

"Good day," said the Mirror. "What can I reflect for you?"

"Oh, I wish to know how I compare to all the other queens," the Queen fretted. "Am I thin enough, bright enough, is my hair silky enough, are my teeth as white? I want to look my best at the Magical Creatures appearance."

"You look lovely, dear Queen," replied the Mirror. "However, I foresee the next magazine cover will show the young Princess Neve. She has a certain something about her. You wouldn't want your big event to be upstaged, would you?"

"Certainly not! But what can I do?" asked the Queen.

The Mirror showed the Queen a magical comb that would age the wearer's hair to a mature silver. "It won't harm the Princess, but magazines won't put silver-haired princesses on their covers. I can have it delivered this very day," the Mirror coaxed.

"I suppose so," said the Queen. "Send it to the Princess then."

Meanwhile in the woods, the gnomes gave Princess Neve a tour of their workshop.

"I've made a pair of laughter slippers that give the user the giggles," said one.

"We're working on a set of wings that humans can use," said two more.

"I'm building a hair-and-beard cutting machine," said one with a lopsided haircut.

"I like your style," said Princess Neve. She helped embellish the wings with silver washers, added a coat of nail varnish to the slippers to give them silly stripes, and even let the gnomes try the hair-cutting machine on her hair. It was fun.

After the tour, Neve found a gift on her pillow. She unwrapped it and discovered it was a hair comb. The Princess popped it in her hair and lay down for the night.

But in the morning Princess Neve woke to quite a surprise. Her hair, once pitch black, was now white as snow. "Huh, that's a new one," Neve said in wonder.

The gnomes gasped. "Do you mind it, Miss? Is it a new trend?"

"Nah. Plus, being off-trend is cool. Call me Snow White!" Neve said with a wink.

Back at the palace, there was only one thing the Queen wanted to know. "How do I look today, Mirror? Will the magazines show me now that the Princess has white hair?"

"Amazing, my Queen!" the Mirror replied. "However, it seems the young Princess has embraced her new do. She's even made up a funny nickname: Snow White. The magazines will probably run with that."

"Seriously?" the Queen sighed. "How am I ever going to capture and keep public favour with Snow White turning every head?"

"Well, there is something you could do. . ."

"What?" asked the Queen eagerly.

"You could tuck her into a deep slumber," suggested the Mirror, "with some fruit from a Charmed Orchard. The young Princess would be preserved like a doll in a glass case, totally unharmed, just asleep. If you want to reverse the spell, all you need to do is touch her forehead and say, 'Rise 'n' shine'. How does that sound?"

"Can you get such an apple, Mirror?" the Queen asked excitedly.

"I thought you'd never ask."

In the woods, Princess Neve and the gnomes were leaving their day at the workshop when Neve noticed a basket by the door with her name on it. Inside was a shiny, red apple. "What a perfect after-work snack," thought Neve and she took a bite. But seconds after that first bite, she fell to the ground.

"What on Earth!" cried the gnomes.

"I think she's asleep," one observed.

Another gnome inspected the fruit. "I think it's this weird apple."

The gnomes carried Princess Neve back to their residence, and laid her in the greenhouse. There Neve slept, comfy as could be.

The Queen turned to the Mirror once again, "Mirror, how do things look for me?"

"With Snow White asleep in the woods, your name and your look will definitely be the headline," the Mirror assured her.

The Queen tried to refocus her energy on her upcoming benefit appearance. But she had trouble concentrating. With the King across the world, and Neve asleep in the woods, the royal residence was lonely. She reviewed the invitation for the Magical Creatures event. It was a costume ball and guests were meant to come dressed as a Magical Creature! The Queen consulted her wardrobe but she had nothing that would work as a costume. She strode past Princess Neve's chambers and noticed a package in the doorway. The box shook a little and she paused.

"It's the Medusa Hair Care kit," the Queen sighed, sitting beside the box which rattled and hissed. "Those snakes are trapped inside." She carefully opened the box and let them loose. The snakes smiled and swirled about, exploring the room.

The Queen looked around her. Neve's walls held posters of royalty from all over the world, riding bikes, eating a pie, grooming unicorns and playing with their families. The Queen's eyes took in Princess Neve's dramatic clothes, bright jewellery and vibrant vanity. All of a sudden it looked inspiring.

The snakes from the Hair Care Kit brought a cerulean scarf, aquamarine glitter and sea-shell hair clips to the Queen's feet and patiently waited for her to fashion them into her hair. Last, but not least, the Queen accentuated everything with glitter.

Feeling stronger and clearer headed, the Queen set off for the woods. "I'll be late to the Magical Creatures event," she told her driver. "We have a stop to make."

When the Queen got to the gnome village, she touched Princess Neve's forehead and said firmly, "Rise 'n Shine." With a yawn, Princess Neve woke to see the Queen.

"What are you doing here?" Neve asked, bewildered. "You look amazing. Are those my Medusa snakes?"

The Queen nodded, "If you don't mind, I'd like to borrow them for the Magical Creatures event and I'd like you to be my date."

"Really?" asked Princess Neve.

"Absolutely," the Queen replied. "Your confidence, the way you celebrate your inner beauty through your playful style – you've shown me that there's no such thing as perfect. I'm trying to raise awareness for important causes, not myself. I've been way too caught up in what other people think," the Queen continued. "The pressure got to me. I'm sorry you got those cruel gifts. I took some bad advice."

"Apology accepted," Neve smiled.

After the Magical Creatures event, the papers carried the following headline: *Queen and Princess announce opening of Inner Beauty Sanctuary*.

From the Inner Beauty Sanctuary in the woods, Neve worked tirelessly on a campaign for real beauty in Fairyland. She also helped ban the creation of enhanced mirrors throughout the kingdom. Meanwhile, the Queen taught seminars on fun with cosmetics. She taught face-painting and woodland-creature hair braiding. She also offered a popular course in weaving, where she repurposed the strings used to cinch the waist. It was called Cinch This!

*"You look amazing. Are those my
Medusa snakes?"*

Evangeline and the Frog Prince

In olden times, when people visited wishing wells regularly, there lived a king with five daughters. Four of them had been recognised for their special talents. One was a celebrated ballerina, the other a brilliant chef who worked magic with knives. Another painted frescoes while balancing on scaffolds in tall towers and the last raced horses while standing atop them! These four princesses were all nimble and deft. Evangeline (Evan), the fifth princess, was different. Evan lacked grace, poise and dexterity. Instead she forever dropped balls, slipped with stacked dishes, bumped into furniture and hit her head on doorways.

Next to the King's castle there was a large, dark forest. In the forest was an old linden tree, and beside the linden tree there was a well. In the forest Evan watched caterpillars, collected lightning bugs and sketched the wildlife that gathered near the linden tree. She spent as much time by the well as she could, trying to wish her woes away and begging for a cure for clumsiness.

"C'mon wishing well, all my sisters are so light-footed and elegant, can't I just have a morsel of that?" Evan pleaded.

After many un-granted wishes, Evan decided to take matters into her own hands. The Princess snuck into her sister's chambers, and helped herself to some of their agility games. A balance beam, a tower of tea cups and a set of gold juggling balls.

The balance beam proved difficult to manoeuvre and Evan always landed with a thud. The stack of tea cups came to a clatter every time she tried to carry them down the hall. "Can you practise that somewhere else?" Evan's sisters yelled. So Evan set off for the linden tree with the set of golden juggling balls.

"Well," she said to the wishing well, "if you can't help me, I'll sort this myself. I'm going to learn how to juggle. That will surely cure my clumsiness."

The golden balls went up, the golden balls went down, and sadly not one landed in Evan's palm. She practised and chased balls all afternoon. Just as the day was nearing to a close, she gave them one last grand toss. Of course, they did not fall into her hands, but instead fell to the ground and rolled right into the well.

"AHHHHHH, grrrrrrr!" Evan stomped her feet and let off steam. "Those were borrowed!" she lamented.

But suddenly she heard a voice from the darkness of the well, "What is the matter, Princess?"

Evan looked closely into the water to see where the voice was coming from and saw a frog. "Oh, hey frog," she said, disappointed. "I'm upset because my sister's golden juggling balls have fallen into the well."

"Not to worry," answered the frog. "I can help you, you'll just owe me a favour."

"Whatever you want. I've a lot of fancy things I never even wear or use as I'm far too clumsy. I could loan you something?"

The frog answered, "I do not want your finery, I'd probably get it all slimy. I'm just looking for a companion and playmate. Maybe I could join you tonight for supper? If you will promise this, I'll dive down and bring your golden balls back."

"Oh, that'd be great," Evan said. "I promise, no problem." But she thought to herself, "My family will surely think I'm uncouth, if I bring home a frog. . ."

As soon as the frog heard her say 'yes', he dove to the bottom of the well. He paddled back up a short time later with the golden juggling balls in his mouth and balanced on his head. The Princess was filled with joy when she saw her sister's items again. She packed them up and ran off, totally forgetting her promise to the frog.

"Wait, wait!" called the frog. "Take me along. I cannot run as fast as you." But Evan had hurried ahead and left the frog behind.

Later that day the Princess sat down to supper with the King and her sisters and all the people of the court. It was a fancy feast so Evan had tucked her napkin round her neck and was trying her best not to spill.

The room was super quiet and everyone could hear the chewing and swallowing, the slurping and the wiping. Then, as she stirred her broth, Evan thought she heard another wet sound. *Drip, drop, drip, drop.* She checked her dish. It sounded like it was coming from outside on the marble steps: *plip, plop, plip, plop.* The sound grew louder and people began to take notice. Soon there came a knock at the door, and a voice called out, "Princess, I've come for supper, is now a good time?!"

"Who could that be?" asked the King. "Evan, see if they'll join us, will you?"

Evan rose from the table and ran to see who was outside. She opened the door, and there on the threshold was the frog, looking hopeful and excited. Panicked, Evan slammed the door shut and returned to the table. The King saw that Evan looked shocked.

"Hey, kiddo, why are you upset, who was at the door? Was it a giant, a troll, a witch or a warlock?"

"Oh, no," she answered. "It's a. . . frog."

Everyone looked puzzled.

"What does the frog want from you?" her sisters inquired.

Evan propped her elbows on the table and launched into an explanation. "But I didn't really think through the promise," she said, at the end of the story. "I didn't think he would actually come. But now he's here, and wants to join us!"

Just then there came a second knock at the door, and a voice called out:

"Young Princess, if you're within,

Open the door would you please,

Don't you recall just this day,

What you said by the well to me?"

The King gave Evan a knowing look, "My dear, we always keep our promises. Go and let the frog in."

Reluctantly, Evan went and opened the door. The frog followed the Princess to her chair, hopped up and drew a napkin to his chin.

The Princess hesitated, until finally the King reminded her to take a seat. With the frog seated in her spot, she lifted him onto the table and sat beside him.

"Now, push your plates closer, so we can all eat together," prompted the King.

The frog enjoyed his meal, but Evan was a little embarrassed. Not only had everyone learned of her misstep, but now she had a frog as her dinner guest. If everyone didn't think she was a royal mess before, she was sure they would now.

But to her astonishment the frog was an elegant guest. He ate heartily and even though he spilled a little, and nearly fell in the dessert, everyone enjoyed his company and welcomed him at the table.

The King could see Evan was troubled. "You should not despise someone who has helped you in a time of need," he whispered. "You two might have more in common than you think."

"But he's a frog, Dad. He's slippery and messy, dripping everywhere and. . ."

"Sounds like someone else I know," said the King, smiling.

Evan sighed, "I suppose you're right."

When the dishes were cleared, Princess Evan picked up the frog, carried him upstairs, and set him on her best pillow.

"I'm sorry if I was rude. I'm not used to having friends over. Tell you the truth, I don't have a lot of princess friends, they are usually off doing more dainty things."

"That's alright," said the frog. "Believe me, I understand. I don't have a lot of friends in the well. I'm a bit of an odd one out myself."

As her guest dozed, the Princess stayed awake and observed him with curiosity.

She noticed he shivered a bit, so she brought him a warming lamp. She noticed his feet were losing their damp, so she quietly crept to the royal library and, by candle light, regarded a reference text which explained how to prepare a foot soak for delicate amphibian feet.

In the morning, the frog slept late. He was so comfortable from all of the special accommodations the Princess had made for him that he woke refreshed and energised.

"You look well," said Evan, as she brought in a tray of breakfast. "I read up on your species' preferences: I have a slippery breakfast broth, snail snacks and fly krispies for sprinkling. Is that to your liking?"

"Wow, that's really cool of you," said the frog, scarfing up the breakfast.

Evan lit up. "Yeah, I learned a lot while you were sleeping. I read a couple of books on amphibians. Your variety is really rare, did you know that?"

The frog laughed, "Yeah, I'll say. If you're interested, I can introduce you to some other exceptional creatures. I know all the lesser-known rainforest bugs, rare birds and a couple of caimans."

"Oh, that'd be so cool," Evan nodded.

And with that, the two packed a backpack for jungle exploring, grabbed a netted hat and hiking boots for Evan and set off for the rainforest. The frog hopped ahead and rattled off facts about endangered and exotic creatures. Over the course of the thrilling day, the frog introduced Evan to a rainbow llama, a near-extinct bat, a cactus spider family, glowing water striders, a luminescent jaguar, twin ostriches and a black-and-white peacock. Evan took copious notes, sketches and asked all sorts of questions about nutrition, sleep patterns and colouring. She was in her element.

When the sun set that evening, the two friends pored over Evan's notes together by the well. "Thanks for a super day," the Princess beamed. "You're welcome to supper with us anytime. You know so much about the animals hidden in our forest. I can't wait to learn more."

"It'd be my pleasure, Princess. I had fun, too. It's so rare to meet people who take such an interest in the inhabitants of the rainforest," said the frog, extending a sticky fist for a knuckle bump.

But Evan went in for a high five and covered the little frog's hand. As the two made contact, a great green lightning bolt shot out from the well and before her very eyes her froggy friend turned into a friendly prince!

"What am I looking at?" inquired the floored Princess. "This wasn't in any of the books."

The Prince laughed, "I'm Prince Pascal. I was enchanted by a wicked witch, and only a person who could see how important even a wee frog could be, would rescue me from life in the well. You're welcome any time to my rainforest kingdom." He bowed deeply with gratitude.

The Princess accepted the generous invitation and would go on to spend many weekends with Pascal, poring over books, specimens and interviewing rare animals that were part of his kingdom.

Evan went on to become a zoologist, who discovered whole new frog species during her work in the rainforest. She and Pascal trekked up great mountains to track the elusive Sapphire butterfly. After learning more about the first-hand experiences of animals, both domestic and wild, Evan campaigned against keeping animals in zoos (magical or otherwise).

She and Pascal trekked up great mountains to track the elusive Sapphire butterfly.

To my lifelong friends, may everyone
be as lucky as I have been - V. M.

To my parents, for their unconditional love - J. B.

Inspiring | Educating | Creating | Entertaining

Brimming with creative inspiration, how-to projects, and useful
information to enrich your everyday life, Quarto Knows is a favourite
destination for those pursuing their interests and passions. Visit our
site and dig deeper with our books into your area of interest:
Quarto Creates, Quarto Cooks, Quarto Homes, Quarto Lives,
Quarto Drives, Quarto Explores, Quarto Gifts, or Quarto Kids.

Power to the Princess © 2018 Quarto Publishing plc. Text © 2018 Vita Murrow.
Illustrations © 2018 Julia Bereciartu.

First published in 2018 by Lincoln Children's Books,
an imprint of The Quarto Group,
The Old Brewery, 6 Blundell Street, London N7 9BH, United Kingdom.
T (0)20 7700 6700 F (0)20 7700 8066 www.QuartoKnows.com

The right of Vita Murrow to be identified as the author and Julia Bereciartu to be
identified as the illustrator of this work has been asserted by them in accordance
with the Copyright, Designs and Patents Act, 1988 (United Kingdom).

A catalogue record for this book is available from the British Library.

ISBN 978-1-78603-202-7

The illustrations were created in watercolour, gouache and coloured pencil
Set in Bembo Roman Infant

Published by Rachel Williams
Designed by Karissa Santos
Edited by Katie Cotton
Production by Jenny Cundill and Kate O'Riordan

Manufactured in Dongguan, China TL122018

3 5 7 9 8 6 4

MIX
Paper from
responsible sources
FSC® C104723
FSC
www.fsc.org